NOBODY'S FOOL

Further Titles from Severn House in this series:

A CORNISH AFFAIR
EVEN CHANCE
LAST RUN
ON WINGS OF LOVE
PLAY FOR LOVE
RAINBOW SUMMER
ROMANY MAGIC
THE ENCHANTED ISLE
THE UNFINISHED

The Dynasty Series:

THE FOUNDING
THE DARK ROSE
THE PRINCELING
THE OAK APPLE
THE BLACK PEARL
THE LONG SHADOW
THE CHEVALIER
THE MAIDEN
THE FLOOD-TIDE
THE TANGLED THREAD
THE EMPEROR
THE VICTORY
THE REGENCY
THE CAMPAIGNERS
THE RECKONING
THE DEVIL'S HORSE
THE POISON TREE

The Kirov Trilogy:

ANNA
FLEUR
EMILY

Detective Novels:

ORCHESTRATED DEATH
DEATH WATCH
NECROCHIP
GRAVE MUSIC
BLOOD LINES

NOBODY'S FOOL

Cynthia Harrod-Eagles

This first world edition published in Great Britain 1997 by
SEVERN HOUSE PUBLISHERS LTD of
9–15 High Street, Sutton, Surrey SM1 1DF.
Previously published in Great Britain in 1980 in
paperback format only under the title *Title Role* and
pseudonym of *Elizabeth Bennett*.
First published in any format in the USA 1997 by
SEVERN HOUSE PUBLISHERS INC. of
595 Madison Avenue, New York, NY 10022.
This edition complete with new introduction from the author.

British Library Cataloguing in Publication Data

Harrod-Eagles, Cynthia
    Nobody's Fool
    1. English fiction – 20th century
    I. Title
    823.9'14 [F]

ISBN 0-7278-4934-4

All situations in this publication are fictitious, and
any resemblance to living persons is purely coincidental.

Typeset by Palimpsest Book Production Limited,
Polmont, Stirlingshire, Scotland.
Printed and bound in Great Britain by
Hartnolls Ltd, Bodmin, Cornwall.

AUTHOR'S NOTE

This novel is one of those which first appeared under the pen-name of Elizabeth Bennett. In re-issuing them under my own name, Severn House has asked me to explain how they came to be written.

People sometime ask me If I always wanted to be a writer, and the truthful answer is that I always *was* a writer – in the sense that I always wrote. Short stories, poems, essays – anything would do, as long as I was putting words together and "telling the tale". When all else failed, or there was no paper (it was still in short supply in my childhood), I carried on a running narrative inside my head about an orphan girl who lived in a cave in the mountains and was befriended by wild animals.

When I reached the grand old age of ten, I began writing my first full-length novel, about an orphan girl who tamed a wild pony (I had two perfectly good parents of my own, and can't imagine why I kept writing about orphans!). When it was finished I began a sequel, and then another. In all I wrote about nine children's novels over my teenage years, and even sent some off to publishers, but they were always rejected, though very kindly.

I went to university and went off ponies a bit when I discovered boys. The result was my first adult novel, which again I submitted to a publisher and had rejected. I changed universities, wrote another adult novel, submitted it – and to my utter astonishment won the Young Writer's Award for it. I had never really believed I would ever be published, but that had never stopped me writing.

Now I held my first published novel, THE WAITING GAME, in my hand, for the first time. It was a wonderful moment.

However, I still had to work for a living, and with a full-time office job, writing had to be squeezed into my evenings and weekends. What happened next was that I was asked by a publisher to write a series of modern romances for them, to order, and in receiving my first commission I felt I had taken an important step in becoming a proper, professional writer. The result was the Emma Woodhouse novels.

Why did I use a pseudonym? Was I ashamed to put my own name on them? Not at all; but in those days publishers believed that if you wrote more than one kind of novel, you had to have a different name for each kind. I was asked to choose a pen-name, and since I happened to be in the middle of my annual re-reading of all the Jane Austen novels, I chose Emma Woodhouse after the heroine of *Emma*. When later another, different publisher commissioned me to write some romances about "career girls", I was obliged to choose another pen-name, and this time, since I was reading *Pride and Prejudice*, I chose the name Elizabeth Bennett.

In course of time the Emma Woodhouse and Elizabeth Bennett books sold out and went out of print, and they have lain dormant ever since. But when, in 1993, I won the Romantic Novelists' Association Novel of the Year Award for my book EMILY, Severn House thought that perhaps my readers might like the chance to see these early works of mine. So here they are, reissued without disguise. I am very glad to see them again in this handsome new edition, proudly flying the banner of my own name this time, and I do hope that you enjoy reading them as much as I enjoyed writing them.

ONE

They were far enough now from the first frantic couplings of their affair to be able to prolong their great mutual pleasure. Dickie paused, pushing himself up on his stretched arms and looking down at her, small and fair against her plum-coloured sheets. The noon sunlight streamed in at the uncurtained window throwing the jumping-diamond reflection of the river on to the ceiling. The house stood by the Thames at Chiswick: they could not be overlooked.

'Is it good?' Dickie asked.

'Mm,' Celia groaned happily. 'Why do you always ask me? Of course it is. Darling – '

'Shh!' he said, freeing one hand to place a finger against her lips. She kissed it and took it between her teeth, and as he began to move again she forgot herself and bit, hard. It drove him to a frenzy. His hands – those long, white hands that she loved – seized two great handfuls of her hair to hold her head still as with fast powerful strokes he brought them both to the climax. Celia heard herself cry out – Dickie never made a sound – and then they collapsed together, sweating a little and breathing hard like runners.

For a few moments Celia was happy. Lying in the post-sexual languor with Dickie's head on her shoulder she knew contentment, she could almost believe that he was entirely hers and she was filling his mind as completely as he filled hers. But comfort like that could not last long: as soon as he spoke, his words would remind her that he was Richard Hayter, the eminent television producer and a married man, and that she, Celia Bancroft, his production assistant, was only having a clandestine affair.

At first she hadn't minded the clandestine side of it. It had been vaguely exciting to exchange secret looks and messages, to meet at prearranged rendezvous, to have the continual spice of anxiety that they might be seen together, recognized. And to do him justice, Dickie had always taken her to expensive places when they went out, and had not expected her to pig it in places as undesirable as they were secret. In fact, everything would have been all right if she had not had the misfortune to fall in love with him.

She hadn't intended to, of course. She had taken the job as production assistant determined only to prove that she was good at it, which she was. But 'nothing propinks like propinquity', and when two talented and attractive people work closely together for long hours something is bound to happen. At first the unspoken attraction had merely added a dimension of secret delight to her working-day and had inspired her clothes-buying, always original, to a pitch of genius. But before long their bodies had begun to react to each other in such a way that if they pored over a script together they practically emitted sparks of static.

Then one day he had tried to squeeze past her in the small space between a filing-cabinet and a desk, and she had turned at the same moment, and one electric second later they were clinging together, kissing frantically.

When it had been revealed to her that Dickie was married – to someone called Margaret who didn't understand him – and had two children of eight and ten, it had seemed the ideal answer to the situation for them to go to her home in the lunch-hours to make love. Celia had been left the house in Chiswick Mall by her parents; she could drive there from the Television Centre in fifteen minutes. Dickie used to say she'd kill them both one day.

A small sound beside her ear made her realize that he had fallen asleep, and she turned her head carefully to look at him, to study the face she knew so well, and loved, from a new angle. From this angle, she thought, his wife – the unknown Margaret – must have looked at him many times; she must be familiar with the delicate shape of the ear; the glitter of close-cropped hair just in front of it, where it turned to silver; the long hollow of the cheek and the deep lines ingrained at the corner of his lips; the droop of the upper lid, softly wrinkled; the gleam along the jawline of the growth of beard since that morning's shave.

Did Margaret watch him shave, she wondered. Did she sit on the edge of the bath and watch him, as Celia would have done? I want to share things with you, she thought. I'm no longer content just to have sex with you. I want to share all your life, wake beside you in the morning and sleep beside you at night. That was the difference falling in love made. Her sexual desire for him was not less, but it was different. Possession of his body was not enough – she wanted his mind, too.

Well, why shouldn't he get a divorce and marry her? He had told her many times that he no longer loved Margaret, and that they didn't sleep together any more. Their marriage was a weary form, gone through for the children's sake, he said. But divorce was a big step. It could not be rushed into. Margaret was not the world's most stable person; the revelation of Celia's existence must be timed carefully if it was not to destroy her.

Celia understood all that. She had no wish to harm Margaret, but if it came to a choice between Margaret's happiness and her own, she had to choose her own. And the situation seemed to be prolonging itself without bringing her any nearer her goal.

She reached across and shook him gently by the shoulder.

'Dickie, darling, wake up. You mustn't sleep now.'

'Uh?' he grunted. He woke painfully, stared at her for a moment with the eye nearest her, and then lifted his head from her shoulder to look at his watch. 'Quite right, we must be going back soon. What about making a quick cup of coffee, darling?'

'That wasn't why I woke you,' Celia said ruefully. 'I just didn't think you ought to waste our time together sleeping.' Dickie was all energy now he had woken. He sat up, slid his legs over the side of the bed, and grabbed for his underpants. Celia did not make any move to get up, but watched him with a vague feeling of dissatisfaction. He was going first to the bathroom to wash, but he would still put on his underpants, just for that. He never walked around entirely naked, though he liked to see her naked. As he stood up he glanced towards his reflection in the full-length mirror, as he always did, and he said, as he always said,

'Not bad for an old man, eh?'

'Very good,' Celia said dutifully. In fact he did have a very good figure for his age, which was forty-five, partly owing to good fortune and partly to ruthless sessions of squash and a weekly visit to the Turkish baths. But his remark today had only drawn Celia's attention to the fact that he was, after all, twenty years her senior, and time was not for them in an endless supply.

'Dickie,' she said suddenly, and firmly enough to halt him on his way to the door. He looked back at her, a little appre-

9

hensively she thought.

'What? And do get a move on, Celia. We only have a few minutes.'

'I know, but – Dickie, don't you think it's time you told Margaret?'

'Told her what?' he asked, playing for time.

'About us,' Celia said patiently. 'I know you don't want to give her a shock but after all, it's going to be a shock whenever it comes, so why wait any longer?'

'Celia, darling, you don't cast off fifteen years of marriage, just like that,' Dickie said with patient amusement.

'I know you don't,' Celia said with rising irritation. 'Nobody's asking you to. But however you do it, you've got to start somewhere. And starting must mean telling her about me. If you don't start, you'll never finish.'

'Of course but – '

'But what? Look, Dickie, I want to marry you and live with you. You're forty-five. I want to have a bit of life with you. The way you're going on you'll be sixty before you've even got around to telling her, let alone getting a divorce.'

'There's nothing like being brutally frank, is there?' he said, offended.

'I wish you would be,' Celia said. 'When are you going to speak to her?'

There was a long silence in which she could almost hear her heart beating as she waited for his answer. He was looking out of the window – anywhere but at her, it seemed – and as the silence lengthened she realized that he was not going to answer. He did not know what to say. He was hoping she would answer for him. The truth came to her, painfully and surely.

'You aren't going to speak to her, are you?' she said. 'You've no intention of getting a divorce or marrying me. You've just been playing around with me, haven't you?'

Now he turned from the window and looked at her. 'Celia,' he began, as if to deny what she had said, and yet with a terrible feeling of doom she saw the relief in his eyes. Until then she had not believed it; even while she had been saying it she had hoped against hope that he would laugh at the idea. But there was no getting round that expression of relief – like a man who dreads a tooth-pulling only to find that the bad tooth has dropped out of its own accord.

'Celia, darling, you know I'm terribly fond of you. You're a wonderful girl – '

'It's okay,' she said flatly. 'Don't bother. I understand everything now. I think we'd better get dressed and back to work, hadn't we? We don't want to be missed, people might start talking.'

'Don't be bitter,' he said pleadingly. 'Don't be bitchy. It isn't you. I always think of you as being so sweet and gentle – '

Celia looked up in amazement. 'You're already talking about me as if I were dead! Listen to yourself. But of course – ' it came to her suddenly – 'but of course, you do. You do listen to yourself, all the time. A life-long performance, Richard Hayter plays Richard Hayter. Perhaps all producers are actors *manqués*; are they, Dickie?'

'Celia – '

'Oh, you know my name? You've been practising.' She jumped up, oblivious of her nakedness, and crossed the room to the chair where her clothes were piled. Dickie watched her, admiration for her body mingling with irritation at the scene he had been forced to take part in. 'Don't worry, I won't make trouble for you, if that's what you're worried about.' Again that faint, give-away gleam of relief. 'I wouldn't give you the satisfaction. Does Margaret know about you? I bet she does. I bet you think you're fooling her every time, but she probably tells her friends about you on their coffee-mornings. "Dickie's got a new girl-friend. The poor dear thinks I don't know about them" – that's what she says. All women aren't as gullible as me, you know. Would you mind dressing in the bathroom – I'd like a little privacy.'

Dickie caught the bundle of his clothes which she flung at him and went silently from the room. Celia felt tears prickling her eyelids, but she would not give way, not now, not when he might see her. She had to get through the rest of the day. She pulled on her clothes, diving through the neck of the yellow linen shirt-waister she had chosen so carefully that morning for Dickie's sake. It smelled, as did all her clothes, of *Tigresse*, the perfume Dickie had first bought her, and which was so inextricably entwined with the thought of him that she knew she would never be able to wear it again. Her life was being broken up into pieces, and when she put it back together, there would be a huge piece missing.

Just as she finished dressing and was picking up her hairbrush to get the tangles out of her long, straight fair hair, Dickie came back into the room. He looked subdued and sheepish, and he spoke to her with a kindness in his voice which made her wonder if after all he might be possessed of a conscience.

'Celia, I'm sorry it has to be this way. But I'm afraid I'll have to ask you to drive me back to the Centre, or I'm going to be late. I hope you don't mind too terribly much.'

'Don't be silly, of course I'll drive you back,' she said briskly. 'You didn't think I'd let you down, did you?' If there was a hint of an emphasis on '*I'd* let *you* down' it was hard to blame her.

Ten minutes later she was driving through the back streets of Shepherds Bush in her navy-blue Aston Martin DB, a car which she had had for years and loved with a consuming passion. She lavished such care and attention on it that it had never let her down, and she mused now that it was the only thing in her life that never had. As she drove, trying to ignore the presence of Dickie beside her, she was thinking that she must get a new job as soon as possible. She was unable to leave until they finished the particular production they were engaged on, but until she could leave, she would feign indifference to him at all costs. She would not give him the satisfaction of seeing her suffer.

It would be hard, of course, to work beside him and never be able to touch him. That would be the most difficult thing. She must tell herself that they had been good in bed together, and that was all. A good bed-partner can be replaced with a little care; there was nothing to be bitter about. She had been a fool to fall in love – Dickie must not have the chance to laugh at her for that.

She dropped him at the front gate of the Television Centre – she would have to drive round to the back to find a parking-space – and as he prepared to get out of the car he opened his mouth to speak, but she forestalled him.

'Please don't say you're sorry,' she said. 'A conflict of aims is nobody's fault.'

'You're a wonderful girl,' he said. 'I really mean that. You're too good for me.' Celia received the compliment coldly. He went on, 'We've done some good work together, and it hasn't just been because we were – what we were to each other. You have great talent, and you should go far.'

'I have an idea how far you'd like me to go,' Celia said, and he had the grace to blush.

'Well, of course, it would be easier if – obviously, it might be less embarrassing – '

'Don't worry, I won't embarrass you. I'll look about for another job. In my own time. And from now on, I think formality would be the best thing, don't you?'

He got out of the car and shut the door. 'Good-bye, Dickie,' she said as she watched him walk away.

By the time the day of the interview came, Celia had decided to accept the job even if it turned out not to be exactly what she wanted, for life in the office had become intolerable. It wasn't so bad when there were other people about, but much of their work was done alone together, and Dickie gave such a good impression of not being unnerved by the situation that it unnerved *her*. She was still attracted to him, and the feeling that her indifference was more of an act than his was depressing.

She had spent the worst Christmas of her life, even including the terrible Christmas when her parents had been breaking up for the first time (they later became reconciled, apparently for the sole purpose of doing it all again), and the possible job with the film company had come up at a time when she really felt she couldn't stand things any longer.

She had taken great care with her appearance, overdrawing herself in order to buy a new suit of chocolate-brown suede which she wore with her best white cashmere sweater and long white boots, a brown leather prairie hat and a brown shoulder-bag; for she felt that she must not fail the interview, whatever the cost. She felt she looked both casual and prosperous, which is what *she* would have wanted an applicant to look like if she were doing the interviewing. She was sorry that the parking problem made it impossible for her to draw up to the door with a flourish in her darling navy-blue car.

The office was in a tiny, narrow, poky-looking house in St Martin's Lane, one of those places with an incredibly seedy front hall in which there are name-plates for each floor giving anonymously familiar names of companies you felt you ought to have heard of: Miranda Productions, Newson Associates, Yates Huxley Ltd, Bantham Films. She had in fact heard of Bantham Films (first floor) and had genuinely admired something they had done only last year – a very artistic black-and-white film about three soldiers in a trench in World War One. She had seen it at the cinema and thought it terrific, and this made her both anxious to tell them so, and worried in case they thought she was only saying it to improve her chances of the job.

The job was producer's assistant, and the producer was called Simon Davis, a name so anonymous that she felt it must be a pseudonym. The company was small, tightly budgeted, and so far, through careful excellence, successful. It sounded very much the kind of thing she would like to be mixed up in, and she was even prepared to take a small drop in salary if that were necessary. Not much of a drop, of course, for though she had no rent to pay, the Chiswick house cost a lot to keep up, and her clothes were a big expense, and she had got used to some of the more extravagant luxuries of life during Dickie's reign.

She reached into her bag for her scent-spray and gave herself a quick refresher course in *Vu* by Ted Lapidus (she had emptied the *Tigresse* down the lavatory on the evening of that last day with Dickie, and had followed it up with some Harpic to get rid of the overpowering smell), and walked up the dirty stone steps to the first floor. A sign on a door deep in the gloom of the unlit landing said 'Bantham Films – Please Walk In', and so she did.

She found herself in a windowless office containing a large number of chairs lined up against the wall, and facing a battered office desk on which there were three telephones, a typewriter and a small mountain of correspondence. Behind the desk sat a young man in a brightly checked shirt. He looked surprised at Celia's entrance, and then said,

'Oh, of course, you must be Miss Bancroft.'

'That's right. How did you know?'

'I was expecting you, of course,' he said.

'You're Mr Davis?'

'Oh no,' he said, as if she ought to have known. 'I'm Bill Bennett, secretary, receptionist and general factotum.' He gestured towards the desk. 'I deal with correspondence and man this place. Simon's hardly ever here, so I'm making the most of today to get lots of letters signed and off. You found us all right then? – well, of course you did,' he answered himself. 'One says these stupid things when one's nervous. But this is such an obscure place, I'm always afraid the Big Chance will pass us by because it can't find us. Still, it is a prestige address, and, believe it or not, it's really very cheap.'

14

'I believe it,' Celia said gravely. He laughed nervously.

'No – I meant – well, you know what property costs in London today. Or perhaps you don't? Oh yes, you are a Londoner – I memorized all your details from your letter so that I could impress you if necessary with my omnipotence.'

'Why would you want to impress me?' Celia asked, puzzled and amused by him.

'You might have turned out to be utterly paralysing – you know the way some television people are, the very richest of the society set, always talking about how poor they are because they haven't any money and then buying everything on Diner's Club and Access and what-not. Would you like some tea?'

'Very much, if it isn't too much trouble.'

'No trouble at *all*,' he said emphatically, as if he really meant it. He tipped his chair on to its back legs, reached his hand behind him and opened the door there a few inches to yell out, 'Simon, she's here!'

'Good,' the voice came back. A brief pause, and then the door was opened and Celia got her first look at her (she hoped) new boss. He was at first glance both pleasant and unalarming, two things she would have stipulated if she had not been so anxious for the job that she was past stipulating. He was a little less than tall, rather stocky, with neat dark hair that was beginning to go grey all over, a rather pale face, with those good, clear-cut features that would have got him type-cast, if he were an actor, as a soldier or a loved and trusted statesman. Celia put his age at around forty, both younger and less dangerous than Dickie. His eyebrows were unexpectedly bushy, and under them his eyes were a bright, almost childish blue. He was smiling with a touch of surprise, and he advanced and offered her his hand to shake.

'I'm Simon Davis. Miss Bancroft, is it? You did ask?' He looked at Bill Bennett.

'Oh yes, it's her all right.' Bill Bennett grinned.

'Why are you both so surprised?' Celia asked. His hand was warm and dry, and he did not immediately relinquish hers.

'We didn't expect you to be so – decorative,' Davis said. 'In our worst moments we thought you'd be either dull and bossy or shrill and supercilious. We didn't imagine anyone with such perfect qualifications could have the added bonus of being so personable. I hope you don't think I'm being rude, but do you always dress like this, or was it a special effort?'

'Oh, about half-and-half,' Celia said airily. She felt she could never take offence at anything he said.

'You'd make an absolutely splendid front-man,' Davis went on. 'You see that we fall a little short on smartness here – ' He waved a hand round the office, and then at himself. He was wearing a suit of dark brown herringbone tweed that had evidently been very expensive when new, and was well-worn and well-loved. 'You'd make such a difference.'

'I have a car like your suit,' Celia said. 'It cost me a fortune, and I've had it for ages, and I adore it.'

Davis laughed. 'You've got a sense of humour too – I really think you're quite perfect. I suppose I shouldn't tell you, but we'd already decided on your qualifications to offer you the job, unless you turned out to be really unbearable, but now I suppose you'll turn *us* down. What sort of car?'

'A DB,' Celia said with the inevitable modest pride. 'Navy-blue, with white upholstery. Flies like an angel.'

'Oh bliss,' he said. 'Come into my office and talk to me. Would you like some tea?'

'Yes, please,' Celia said for the second time.

'It's all right, I'll make it,' Bill Bennett said. Celia liked the implication of this, that it might very well *not* have been him who made it. She liked people who weren't so rank-conscious they threw up their hands in horror at the idea of performing a task they thought below them.

'I'd love some tea,' Celia said, 'and since we're being frank, I'd also like the job, if you want to offer it to me.'

'Oh no,' Davis said anxiously, 'you mustn't let me shame you into accepting it until you've had time to think and ask questions. Bill, remind me not to be disarmingly frank with people.'

Bill pretended to note it down. 'No disarming frankness,' he intoned. Celia laughed.

'Really, I'd love to work for you. I saw *Death of a Patriot* last year, and I thought then that it was exactly the kind of film I'd like to be involved with, given the chance.'

'Did you really like it? I must say I was very happy with it myself, though one doesn't often come across that kind of script.' He led Celia into his office, which was smaller than the outer office, but had a window which looked out on to St Martin's Lane, and curtains, and a carpet with no holes in it. Two pigeons were sitting on the sill outside the window, half-obscured by the dust on the panes, their heads sunk into their bodies in sleep. Davis held a chair for Celia, kindly and superfluously, until she sat, and then took his own chair.

'Now about salary,' he said, and named a figure so much higher than what she was getting that she repeated it in a dim sort of way. 'Too little?' Davis asked anxiously, watching her face. 'I'm afraid we truly can't manage any more on our present budget.'

'It's much more than I'm getting,' Celia said. 'I accept, before you change your mind and realize you've offered too much.'

'I'm surprised you think it's a lot. Television mustn't be paying too well. How on earth do you manage to dress so beautifully on so little? – don't answer that. Davis, mind your own business. Well, since that part's all right, let's talk about the work. We're just finishing off a film at the moment – my last assistant left in a hurry – '

Oh my God, not another one, Celia thought, and her face must have shown it because he stopped in mid-sentence and said, 'What's wrong?'

'Why did she leave in a hurry?' she asked. He looked relieved, and then laughed.

'Oh, I see. Nothing like that. I must strike charm from my list of behaviour patterns, if that's the effect it has on you. No, my assistant was a *he*, and he left because his wife had just got promoted to a job down in South Wales. He's gone into regional television, I believe – another good man gone west. You can travel, I take it? No cats, dogs, husbands or children that can't be left?'

'None of any of them,' Celia said.

'That's good. We're away a lot, of course. We're filming down at Salisbury at the moment, and as soon as that's done we'll have to start location-filming on our next production, so you can see we've got a tight schedule.'

Bill came in at that moment with the tea, put the tray down on the desk, and drew up a chair for himself. 'Shall I be mother?' he asked whimsically, crooking a little finger as he lifted the teapot.

'That's the trouble with rubbing shoulders with actors most of the time,' Davis said, shaking his head sadly. 'Camp as a row of tents, most of them, and it rubs off. You're nothing of an actor, I suppose?' he asked Celia.

'Nothing,' Celia said firmly.

17

'Thank God for that. The trouble with actors is you can never tell when they've stopped acting, if indeed they ever do. I suspect not. Bill was in rep for two years and it almost destroyed him as a human being.' Bill smiled unconcernedly, passing Celia her cup, which didn't match its saucer, nor anything else on the tray.

'Now then, Miss Bancroft,' Davis went on, adding wistfully, 'I suppose it's too early to call you Celia?'

'Not if I can call you Simon,' she said.

'I'd prefer it to Celia,' he said. 'Drink up your nice tea, and then if you haven't got anything else planned for this afternoon, you can come along with me to the cutting-rooms and look at the rushes of *Long After Midnight* – that's the present piece of nonsense. Rather in the vein of the Supernatural series you did with Richard Hayter – I've done my homework, you see. And then – '

'Does this mean that I've got the job?' Celia interposed. He looked surprised.

'But of course. I'd thought we'd gone through all that. Now then, after the cutting-room we can go and get some grub somewhere, and we can have a look at the script of our next little adventure together. We'll go somewhere festive, and combine work with a celebration of our mutual good fortune. Bill can't come, unfortunately – he's got a wife-and-two to go home to. Do you like sea-food?'

'Yes,' Celia said – all she managed to get in.

'We'll go to Wheeler's then, and afterwards you can drop me off at my place on your way home. I live in Kensignton, so I won't be taking you out of your way. It must be ten years since I was inside an Aston Martin. You'll have to tie me down to stop me taking the wheel from you.'

He smiled at her so pleasantly that she could neither object to his plans nor doubt his intentions. He was, she felt, simply and completely a nice person, certainly no threat to her peace of mind. He would treat her as a colleague, just as he treated Bill Bennett; and the job would be fun, and the travel, and this time she would make sure she didn't get off on the wrong foot. She was only sorry she had to work out a month's notice, for she would have been glad never to see Dickie Hayter again.

TWO

Celia's friend, Eva Taunton, came over to spend one Saturday afternoon with her for, as she put it, 'girl-talk, rest and general resuscitation'. Eva was a top make-up artist at the BBC. She and Celia had been friends for a long time, having once shared a flat, and in fact it was Eva who had pointed out to Celia the advertisement for the job as Dickie's assistant and suggested that she apply for it.

Eva was a tall, handsome girl with expansive gestures, and as soon as she arrived she kicked off her shoes and spread herself on Celia's Chesterfield with a huge sigh.

'Oh Celia, what bliss! I don't think I've been off my feet for a week. How marvellous this place is – I always forget each time how lovely the view over the river is. Is it too cold to have the doors open? I just love that rank river-smell you get here.'

'No, I don't think it's too cold. Anyway, if it is I can always shut them again,' Celia said, crossing to the french windows and pushing them open. Beyond them was a small, wrought-iron balcony, and beyond that a small strand and the river. The opposite bank was green and tree-studded, and the tangled overgrowth of Chiswick Eyot hid some nearby buildings from view. 'I always think,' Celia said, 'that this must be almost what the river looked like in the old days, when Chiswick was a riverside resort people from London went to for their summer holidays.'

'Almost, darling,' Eva said wryly, 'apart from the distant tower-blocks and the sweet sound of jumbo-jets up in the sky.'

'You have no poetry in your soul,' Celia smiled. 'Can I get you a drink?'

'Oh yes, please – one of your exotic mixes?'

'If you like. You just relax – I'll be back in a minute.'

She was, with large dew-beaded tumblers of yellow liquid, decorated with slices of orange and cucumber and cocktail cherries, and clinking with ice. The drink was one of her own devising, the main ingredients of which were white rum and pineapple juice.

'Wot, no knife and fork?' Eva joked, eyeing the crowded

glass. 'It looks heavenly, darling. What a wonderfully expensive sound ice makes in a glass!'

'Now then,' Celia said, settling herself on the floor near her friend, 'tell me about your hectic week. What have you been doing?'

'It's been murder, darling,' Eva said. 'Pure homicide. We've been finishing off the Malborough series. Fifty wigs! And everyone ages twenty years in the last episode – I was knee-deep in crow's feet and foam-rubber dewlaps!' Eva's speciality was period drama, and she was very highly thought of.

'I'm dying to see it,' Celia said. 'When's it going to be on?'

'Beginning of June, if all goes well, and I don't see why it should. There never was such a star-struck production – it's been one mishap after another. Mind you, it's nothing to what's happened to poor Julie. I don't suppose you heard about that, did you?'

Julie Harper was another friend of them both, also a make-up artist at the Television Centre.

'No, what?' Celia asked.

'Well, you know she was in charge of the *Sense and Sensibility* production? She's been booted off.'

'No!'

'Yes, the poor girl fell foul of egomania in its most rampant form. Lead actor, God rot him!'

'Who was it?'

'Maxwell Prior.'

'Really? I thought he was a nice bloke.'

'All sweetness-and-light to the right people, darling, but thinks the service crews are underlings – you know the sort,' Eva said, contemplating her bare toes. 'Julie had five people under her and moustaches and eyebrows to do as well as wigs, and you know what it's like in those make-up rooms during the dress-runs.' Celia nodded. 'Well then Prior takes it to mind that he's too important to walk about the corridors in his didies, and sends out a royal command for Julie to come and make him up in his dressing-room.'

'And Julie refused?'

'She did more than that. The word came when she was elbow-deep in bearded extras, and she saw red. She dropped everything and marched along to his room, and told him that there was only one person she'd make up in his dressing-room, and that was only so that he didn't get blood on the carpets from the holes in his feet.'

'She must have been furious,' Celia said. 'Julie's usually the most patient of people. What happened?'

'With the Prior? Well he didn't say anything then – I suppose he was too stunned – these egomaniacs are often cowards at heart. Instead he went to the director behind Julie's back and said it was her or him.'

'I can imagine what the director said,' Celia nodded grimly.

'Of course. Prior was his blue-eyed boy. So they shoved Julie off and gave the job to Faye Madison, who, bless her, is a good make-up artist but hopeless at admin, poor pet, and could no more cope with five girls under her than fly in the air. She couldn't organize a screw in a whorehouse, so the make-up will be lousy, but what director ever cared about anything but his own misunderstood genius? They think make-up and wigs do themselves.'

'So this Prior is a bit of a bastard, then?' Celia asked thoughtfully. She had seen him in quite a few productions, both television and film, and had thought highly of him. She thought him a talented actor, and his looks were of the kind that appealed to her – the dark, romantic type.

'Aren't they all, darling.' Eva dismissed him lightly. 'And talking of bastards, your own particular ex-bastard seems to be getting his come-uppance. But there, if you will go playing with hot wax, you're bound to get your fingers burned.'

'I presume you're talking about Dickie?' Celia said awkwardly. One part of her longed to hear about him, even to have his name mentioned, while another part of her wanted to shun the memory that he even existed. Eva nodded and went on,

'Yes, old hot-lips is at it again. This time he's got himself involved with a scenic artist, one of those dolly-bird drop-outs from the Chelsea School of Art with legs that go up to their chins. She wears Andy-Pandy dungarees and nothing else – you know the type.' Celia nodded carefully, trying not to let the pain show. 'I think this time it's different, though – the poor sap seems to be making a fool of himself. Everyone's talking about him – he hangs about her like a sick spaniel and she treats him like dirt. I think this time he's really fallen at last – unbelievable as it may seem for a hardened old cocksman like Dickie Hayter.'

Celia nodded again, and then said, 'Poor Dickie. I never

realized – I mean, did you know all along he was like that? Having affairs, I mean?'

'That's putting it mildly, darling,' Eva said. 'Everyone knew about Dickie's proclivities.'

'And yet you never warned me,' Celia said reproachfully. Eva swung her legs off the Chesterfield and impulsively took one of Celia's hands, her flippancy gone for a moment.

'Celia, what good would it have done? You were madly in love with him, and if I'd said anything along those lines you wouldn't have believed me, and I'd have lost a friend into the bargain. You'd have thought I was jealous or something. I trusted to the fact that sooner or later everyone finds out that Dickie is completely hollow inside, and you can't be seriously hurt by anything as shallow as that.'

'I don't know about that,' Celia said slowly. Eva pressed her hand.

'I do. You aren't badly hurt. You're too good a person to be wounded by the worthless. Your only fault is this delightfully old-fashioned way you have of falling in love with your lovers. But you'll grow out of it.'

'I don't know that I will,' Celia said, releasing her hand and reaching for her drink.

'Of course you will, my pet. You don't have to *be* in love to *make* love, you know – it can be fun and nothing else. Every girl goes through someone like Dickie – he's like an education service, really; one should be grateful for him. But once you've graduated from Dickie, the world starts to open up, and the fun really starts. Don't take anything too seriously, Celia. Really, I'm terribly sorry for the poor old sod, because he seems to have got to the age when he's going to start on the nymphette bit, and that's the beginning of the end.' She looked carefully at Celia, and judged a change of subject necessary. 'But tell me, how are you getting on with your new job? What's the new boss like to work for?'

'He's very nice. We get on very well, as if we've known each other for years,' Celia said, dragging herself out of the unpleasant memories of the past. Eva's eyebrow raised itself. 'No, not like that,' Celia said hastily. 'I'm not so stupid as to throw myself into the frying-pan when I've just got burnt by the fire. He's not like that at all. He's completely neutral. The three of us work together as colleagues.'

'Three of you?'

'His secretary.'

'What's she like?'

'He. It's a him. A man by the name of Bill Bennett, terribly nice again.'

'Oh.' Eva considered this. 'Are they gay?'

'No, of course not,' Celia said at once. 'Why should you think so?'

'Two men working together, and the fact that they apparently haven't made any passes at you.'

'I told you, it isn't like that,' Celia said, annoyed. 'Besides, Bill's married. With two children.'

'And the other one? What is his name, anyway?'

'Simon. Simon Davis.'

'Oh, I've heard of *him*,' Eva said with respect. 'Is he married?'

'I don't know. I've never asked, and he's never mentioned it. I presume not.'

'Probably divorced, then,' Eva said, settling it to her own satisfaction. 'Look, darling, what are you doing tonight?'

'I was going to have a bath, wash my hair, and then get into bed with the script I've got to read.'

'All right, well have your bath, wash your hair, and then come out with me to a party. You need some diversion. I see the telltale signs of a decline approaching.'

'Evie, I really do have to read this script. We're having a meeting with the director on Monday to discuss it.'

'Oh aren't we grand! But you can read the jolly old script tomorrow, darling – a girl with a brain like yours can master a script in a day. Never give up present pleasure for the prospect of future virtue. Look what happened to the Christian martyrs.'

'Eva –'

'Now, now, I insist. Listen to your aunty's good advice. I've got the offer of a couple of parties, and I'll choose the raviest, and you shall wear your very best frock with the smocking and the butterfly bows, and I shall personally conduct you to a good time. I'll get Sandy to come with us, and then he can worry about keeping sober to drive us home.'

'Well, I don't know –'

'Yes you do! You'd like an evening out. I'll bet you haven't been out since old creepy last invested a dinner in your beautiful body. Make yourself look ravishing, and we'll go and rave. It will do your bruised ego good to have a few smart young men leching over you. You needn't do anything about them, you know, if you don't want to!'

'Oh Eva.' Celia laughed at last. 'You're impossible. All right, I'll come.'

'And enjoy yourself?' Eva added warily. 'No martyred sighs?'

'I promise to do everything I can to enjoy myself.'

'That's a good girl. You *shall* go to the ball, Cinderella, and not wiv no bleedin' rat for a coachman, neiver!'

Eva called for her at nine, accompanied by her semi-permanent lover Sandy, who was a news editor on the World Service, a dignified Scots ex-Guardsman with beautiful manners and an unexpected fund of filthy stories.

'I thought we'd go to Toby Llewellyn's,' Eva said. 'Her drinks are better than Paul Harris's, and her guests are no worse. There are bound to be some fairly hot people there; it'll take you out of yourself, dearie. I must say, Celia, you've done me proud tonight. You look sensational.'

'Thank you,' Celia said, smiling. 'We aim to please, ladies and gents.' She had taken extra care and was glad she won her friend's approval. She had chosen, after long consideration, dark cerise silk beach-pyjamas with a plunging front and hardly any back to speak of, which she was wearing with some very tarty pink high-heeled sandals and several heavy gold chains around her throat. Her shining hair fell like four feet of pale water down her back. 'Do we have to take a bottle with us?'

Eva shook her head. 'No, darling, it isn't that sort of party. Is it Sandy?'

'Should think not,' Sandy grunted, amused. 'Toby's married to Boris Szralko. Don't you know about Boris? He owns everything in London the Arabs don't. Filthy rich. That's why their drinks are better – not that I shall have the opportunity to find out.'

'Now Sandy, you *offered* to drive us,' Eva said coaxingly. He gave Celia the ghost of a wink.

'Course I did, m'dear. I remember you telling me so.'

Celia was surprised to find herself, when she got out of Sandy's car, in the same street as the one in which she had dropped Simon Davis on that first day when she had driven him home. The party was in one of the large, beautiful service-flats with which the area round Kensington High Street abounds.

'My boss lives along here,' she told Eva.

'I'm not surprised,' Eva said. 'There are lots of film people around here. Funny how types seem to stick together.'

'How do you come to know these people?' Celia asked as they walked up to the front door.

'I used to make up Toby years ago when she was modelling,' Eva said. 'We liked each other, and we've kept in touch in a loose sort of way. She moves in a very high-powered set now, since she married Boris, but she's good fun. I don't know what her guests will be like tonight, but if we don't like it we can always go on to Paul Harris's.'

They went up in the beautifully ornate old lift and a few moments later were inside the flat. There was a tremendous din of music and voices, and everywhere moved crowds of beautifully dressed people talking and drinking and dancing and generally enjoying themselves, some of them in some very odd ways. Sandy steered them with practised ease through the throng until they met their host and hostess. Toby was a tall, elegant woman who had once been stunningly beautiful and was still very good-looking, though her south-of-France tan made her skin look very tired. She was clutching a nasty little white toy poodle in a jewelled collar.

'Evie darling! And Sandy! So glad you could come.'

'Hello, Toby. This is my friend Celia Bancroft, who needs cheering up.'

Someone squeezing past them at that moment forced Celia up against her hostess so that she found herself practically nose-to-nose with the poodle. The dog stared at her with the blank eyes of a life-prisoner, and then began to bark in a mechanically hysterical way.

'This is Cascara,' Toby said, shaking the dog to shut it up.

'Cascara?' Celia queried, wondering if she'd heard wrong or if Toby didn't know the meaning of the word.

'We called him that because when we first got him he shat non-stop, everywhere. We had to completely re-carpet the flat to get rid of the smell, didn't we, Boris?'

Boris grunted. He appeared to be at least twice Toby's age, and rather frail, though he had the same tan as his wife.

'This is my husband Boris, by the way.' Toby introduced him to Celia. 'He's a nasty, lecherous old man, but he's horribly rich, aren't you, Boris? He loves Cascara. He didn't mind the shit at all. He said it reminded him of his children when they were babies. Have you people got drinks? I hope you don't want me to introduce you because, frankly, I haven't a clue who half of these people are. I invited Christopher, and he's been terribly naughty and asked a whole lot of his friends, and they've invited *their* friends, none of whom I've ever met. You can easily tell them, though – they're all terribly gay. Some of them are doing yoga in the drawing-room – that's what all that dreadful Indian music is for.'

'When did Christopher get back?' Eva asked when she could get a word in.

'I've no idea, darling,' Toby said, 'but we saw him last Sunday. I really rather hoped it would turn out that he was the mystery tourist that got busted for drugs in Turkey, but no such luck. He came home trailing the most dreadful male prostitute that he'd picked up in the Bosphorus, but Boris came the heavy father and turned him out, didn't you Boris?'

Boris grunted again. He did not seem a conversational man, and Celia wondered if it was congenital, or a result of living with Toby.

'Who's Christopher?' Celia asked Eva when they had left Toby to get drinks and circulate.

'Christopher Shalako,' Eva elucidated.

'The actor?' Celia asked in surprise.

'Yes. He's Boris's son by his first wife. Changed the family name into something a little more pronounceable. He had an affair with Toby just after she married Boris, and then he got into all sorts of trouble and practically had to leave the country. Toby can't stand him – she doesn't like homosexuals, and Christopher's bi, but more homo than hetero, and I think she resents the way he runs through Boris's money.'

'It's rather off-putting to hear these horrible facts about people you admire,' Celia said. 'I saw him in *Death of a Patriot* and thought he was terrific. So other-worldly and pure.'

Sandy laughed. 'It's another world altogether *he* inhabits. Other-worldly is right.'

'Of course,' Eva said. 'He was in *Death of a Patriot*. I'd forgotten. Your Simon Davis must know him. I wonder – '

'Stop adding two and two,' Celia said quickly.

'And getting twelve,' Sandy added.

26

'I was only going to say I wonder why he chose Christopher for that role,' Eva said.

'I know you were. And I've told you, Simon isn't. And anyway, he didn't choose him. You ought to know as well as I do that it's the director who casts the leads.'

'I know, I know, but with an outfit like Bantham, you can't try and tell me that Simon Davis doesn't have a big fat say in who gets what part,' Eva said. 'A director isn't likely to go too far against the man who puts up the money almost single-handed.'

'Even if he did, he would have chosen Shalako for his acting ability,' Celia retorted hotly, 'and you can't say it didn't work well. Everyone said Shalako was perfect for the role.'

'Darling, don't get so upset,' Eva said, raising her eyebrows. 'You're defending your boss like a faithful little terrier. I do hope I don't detect the first little spots in a rash of new love?'

Celia pulled herself up. Perhaps she had been too fervent. 'No, no,' she said calmly. 'Nothing like that. It's just that I don't like all this casual condemning of people as homosexuals that goes on nowadays. Anyone who isn't married seems to be fair game.'

'Don't be silly, darling,' Eva said, giving Celia a quick hug. 'Nobody's condemning anybody. Some of my best friends are homosexuals. And some of my best friends aren't, are they Sandy?' She said the last words in an imitation of Toby's 'Are they, Boris?' and Sandy, quick on the uptake, replied with Boris's grunt, which made Celia laugh. 'Let's have a look round,' Eva suggested. 'We've got to circulate Celia's bare back or she'll never bring down the overheads on that outfit.'

One or two of the faces around her seemed familiar to Celia, and she guessed that they were film people whose faces she had seen on the screen or in newspapers. In the drawing-room there was a Ravi Shankar record on the player, going full blast along with the sweet stink of joss-sticks, and several people were holding yoga positions while a lot more sat or lounged about looking on. One rather pretty small woman was doing supported ballet holds with her hand held by a golden-haired young man whom Celia recognized at once as Christopher Shalako, and she remembered from some long-ago-read article that he had been in training for the ballet when he had been chosen for his first starring role, in *The Stone Man*, after which he had never looked back.

Celia looked at him with some interest. He had an interesting, rather than a handsome, face, a long, thin body, redeemed from weediness by the strong shoulders and arms of a ballet dancer, and bright blond hair that Celia, with a natural blonde's keen eye, surmised to be dyed. He was wearing pale pink jeans and a fluffy, powder-blue sweater; his eyes were half-closed as he took the positions and supported the girl dancer with easy, manipulative strength; his sculptured profile looked strong and sensitive. She could not draw any conclusions from him, but the memory of Simon Davis's kindly, very human face made her feel ashamed even to have wondered for a moment whether he could have been motivated by anything so base as a desire to get this enigmatic creature into bed.

They passed on into another room where the atmosphere was purer and the noise level more tolerable, and here Eva and Sandy met up with some BBC friends and got settled into a pleasantly chatting circle. Celia didn't know any of them, but she listened at first and joined in a little as they talked about things she knew to do with the BBC; but after a while the fact that she was now out of it began to show, and she grew a little tired of shop-talk. Her attention wandered, and she found herself watching a little cameo on the other side of the room, of two remarkably attractive young women talking to a man whose back, which was towards Celia, was somehow distantly familiar.

Celia could not hear what was being said, but from the expressions on the girls' faces and their movements and attitudes, it seemed plain that they were both attempting to impress or get off with the man, and that he was giving neither of them a lead over the other. Celia found herself instinctively disliking the man, although there was no reason why she should, since evidently no one was forcing the two girls to compete in that undignified way. But there was something about his stance and the carriage of his dark-haired head that suggested he thought himself no end of a bucko, for whom any girl in her right mind would compete.

Girl Number One was being languishing, and Girl Number Two was being vivacious. Celia wondered in momentary depression whether anyone ever behaved naturally any more, or married someone they loved and stayed with them for ever. After all, look at the messes around her: there was Eva, unmarried and intending never to marry, and Sandy, twice-divorced, coming back to each other in the intervals of screwing other people; Toby marrying an old man for his money and having an affair with his

28

son; Dickie, making it with a succession of assistants while his wife waited patiently at home, and finally falling for an art-school dolly who despised him. It seemed that nowadays it was an absurd anachronism to want to marry for love and stay married. Sex was fun, but didn't there come a time when you wanted something more, a little companionship perhaps?

She was still thinking along those lines when the man whose back she was staring at absently turned round and caught her eye. His face was familiar, and thinking she knew him she had just begun to smile when she realized who he was. It was the actor, Maxwell Prior. Instantly she clamped down on the beginning of the smile she had been about to give him, and turned her head away, back to the conversation she should have been a part of. As she looked away, she saw, or thought she saw, him raise his eyebrows in surprise. When she glanced back again a moment later, a surge of bodies had closed the gap between the two groups, and she could not see him at all.

THREE

The party had livened up as far as Celia was concerned, for several people had asked her to dance, and she had been thoroughly 'chatted up' by her dancing partners. Wherever she was in the room dancing, there was a small group of young men watching, and Celia found that Eva was quite right, that a little flirtation and flattery is very good indeed for the bruised ego. Apply three times daily after meals, she thought. Her pink pyjamas and naked back were attracting all the attention she wanted just then.

After several strenuous dances-cum-fencing-matches, she escaped to the loo, among other things to make sure nothing had come adrift and to mop up any unlady-like sweat. She re-brushed her hair, retouched her make-up, put on a little more scent, and emerged a new woman, into the arms, almost literally, of Maxwell Prior.

'Ah, there you are!' he exclaimed. Celia glanced behind her, but he seemed to be addressing her.

'Me?' she said, puzzled.

'The dancing has lost some of its zing since you disappeared. I was hoping you hadn't gone home.'

'I just went to the loo,' Celia said foolishly, proving once again that there is no limit to the daft things you can say when caught off-balance. Prior wisely ignored the gaffe – he had his own copy of the script to follow.

'Don't I know you from somewhere?' he asked with stunning originality.

Celia smiled inwardly as a number of retorts sprang to mind, but in fact all she said was, 'No.'

'So definite?' Prior said, an eyebrow raised quizzically. 'Don't you know me?'

'No,' Celia said again, answering the literal rather than the implied question, and then added, for honesty's sake, 'When I nearly smiled at you in there it was because I thought for a minute I knew you, but of course it was only because I recognized you. I'm sorry.'

'Sorry?'

'You must be tired of complete strangers saying hello to you all the time.' He still looked as if he didn't understand, and, like a mug, Celia ploughed on, 'I once passed Frank Bough in the street, and his face was so familiar that I smiled and said hello, thinking it was someone I knew from somewhere, and it was only when I was about to stop and speak to him that I realized who he was, and I felt such a fool. I just went bright red and scuttled away. But on afterthought he must have been less surprised than I was, since it must be happening to him all the time – as it must to you,' she finished, almost breathless.

'Not all that often,' Prior said. 'I wouldn't mind if it happened more often, if it was with beautiful women like you.'

The standard line Celia could recognize even from a disadvantageous position, and there was nothing more likely to annoy her. She had been chatted up by four different young men in varying degrees of originality and had accepted the compliment that was intended, but it irritated her to think that Maxwell Prior thought that because he was a Famous Film Star he didn't have to try any harder than that. At that point in *his* script she was supposed to melt at his subtle flattery and giggle and say coyly, 'Ooh, do you really think I'm beautiful, Mr Prior?'

Instead she stared at him coldly, said, 'There aren't any beautiful women *like* me. I am unique. Excuse me – ' and tried to pass him. He put his hand up on the wall and lounged against it, blocking her way, *à la* cowboy film *circa* 1956.

'I'm beginning to think you could be right,' he said insinuatingly.

'Lady,' Celia said impatiently.

'Eh?' Prior fell out of role for the moment it took to be puzzled.

' "I'm beginning to think you could be right, *lady*",' she said. 'For God's sake, if you're going to act like a bad film, get the clichés right.' She was surprised with herself the moment she said it. It was the rudest she had ever been to anyone, and it was fairly unprovoked. Prior evidently felt he hadn't deserved it. He straightened up sharply, removing his arm from her path, and was just about to say something very cold and cutting when a long serpentine arm curled around him from behind, and one of the beautiful women he had been talking to in the other room cooed seductively,

'Maxie *darling*, where have you been? You've been such an *age* – I thought you were going to get me another drink.' She flashed a malevolent and warning glance across his shoulder at Celia. Prior gave Celia one more hard glare, and then turned to his companion and switched on a charming smile.

'Of course 1 was, Poppy my sweet. Come along now, and I'll get you some champagne.'

'Oh *thank* you, Maxie darling,' Poppy sighed, gazing up at him with enraptured gratitude as if he was proposing to scale the Tibetan heights to bring her back some lost treasure. Celia had been feeling a little uncomfortable with herself, but as Maxie darling and Poppy my sweet moved away, arms entwined, she smiled to herself at the ludicrous contrast between his cold glare and the soupy sweetness he turned on Poppy, no doubt for the purpose of impressing her as to what she had given up for the want of a little politeness and humility.

A moment later she had rejoined Eva and Sandy and their group.

'Where have you been, Celia darling?' Eva asked her, putting an arm round her to bring her into the group.

'Oh, just outside being rude to Maxwell Prior.'

'Oh, well, good for you, darling,' Eva said. 'After what he did to poor Julie, that little poop had it coming.'

Celia had forgotten that Prior was the villain of that piece. Well, it fitted. Humility obviously wasn't *his* vice.

'I was just going to come and find you, actually,' Sandy said, smoothing his non-existent moustache, which was a gesture he had when he was nervous. 'I wondered if you could bear to dance with a balding old soldier?'

'Certainly, if you've got one handy,' Celia said quickly, and Sandy laughed.

He led her to the place where people were dancing, and as he took her into his arms he sighed happily and said, 'I wish some-one was on hand with a cine-camera. I'd like to have a permanent record of the evening I danced with a beautiful woman in backless pyjamas.'

Celia smiled indulgently. There it was, you see – the same sort of thing from Sandy wasn't at all insulting, proving the validity of the old saw: that it ain't what you do, it's the way that you do it. Amen.

*

She slept late on Sunday, and then, after a light, late breakfast, she took a long, slow bath to get the smell of smoke out of her skin. Bathing was a pleasure she took seriously, the one pleasure, she thought, that one could never tire of. She lounged back in the water, scented with Floris bath oil, cleansed her skin with Guerlain soap, sipping from time to time at a tall glass of iced orange juice, and listening to Joan Armatrading on her portable tape-recorder. Afterwards, she wrapped herself in a huge, deep-piled bathsheet and patted herself dry, and then, letting her hair down out of her shower-cap, she padded naked into the bedroom to brush it out before the mirror.

It was there that she was suddenly overcome by a feeling of melancholy. She brushed and brushed at her long, moon-coloured hair, and stared at herself in the mirror, and wondered what it was all about. An attack of *weltschmerz*, she told herself (what Steinbeck called Welsh Rats), brought on by a late night and too much booze. And yet – there she was, a beautiful young thing, a shapely body, lovely hair, pretty face, and where had it got her? Men had wanted her, had taken pleasure from her, but what had she ever got from it? She wondered just how much pleasure she had ever got from sex; perhaps it was all in the mind. She had always had to be in love before she desired a man enough to want sex with him, and then, being in love, the sex had seemed wonderful.

Eva said she was hopelessly old-fashioned, that sex could be enjoyed for itself without a lifetime's committment. But if she was not built that way, what hope was there for her? None of her lovers had intended anything permanent by their relationships; perhaps it was absurd in this enlightened age to want a long standing, meaningful relationship with a person; perhaps 'love' really only existed between the covers of silly romance novels. If that was what she wanted, she was doomed to disappointment. She had better start trying to find out about the pleasures of sex-without-love, and console herself with the thought that, if she did find the perfect person and get married, she might find that *she* tired of *him* after a few years.

That evening, when Celia had gone through the script until she was almost cross-eyed and was thinking of turning in, Eva rang to see how she was and if she had enjoyed her evening.

'It was intended to be therapeutic, so if you don't feel better, I may have to repeat or even increase the dosage,' Eva said.

'Maybe the medicine isn't the right one,' Celia suggested.

'Oh dear, what's the matter? You sound glum. You can't have a hangover – Toby's booze is of the very best quality, nothing but first-class meths served here.'

'I had the blues,' Celia said. 'Had, in the past tense. I was thinking on the mutability of love and the transience of human relationships.'

'Blimey,' Eva said, 'no wonder you went under! Listen, my child, and take it from your Aunty Eva, the only answer is variety and plenty of it. All too soon age will creep up on you and you'll find you have neither the will nor the equipment. Enjoy the display in the supermarket while you've still got money in your purse.'

'I get the general idea,' Celia protested. 'No more extended metaphors, please. There were enough of them in this blasted script.'

'Oh yes, the famous script. No good?'

'It reads like Patience Strong, but then I suppose it was never meant to be read. Terribly symbolic, with a capital "s", you know the sort of thing. Little men walking down big roads, couples silhouetted on a beach at sunset. But most of those passages will make very feasible montage, and – '

'Woah!' Eva cried. 'No more. I didn't phone to talk shop with you, my treasured one, just to make sure you enjoyed your little adventure into the land of naughties last night.'

'I didn't actually do any naughties,' Celia reminded her.

'No more you did. Still, your turn will come, never fear, and when it does, remember your Aunty Eva's aphorism.'

'What's that?'

'That all men are fun for a night; most men are fun for a month; some men are fun for a year; but no man is fun for life.'

'Thanks,' Celia said ironically. 'That was just the sort of advice I've been searching for all day.'

It felt rather strange the next day to be returning to the scene of the party: the meeting was to be held at Simon's flat which, of course, was in the same street as Toby Llewellyn's. Celia had dressed very carefully that morning, for the director Simon had got for his next production was Walter Bruno, and, apart from his reputation as a brilliant director, he also had a reputation as a dilettante. The thought of meeting him would be less daunting, she felt, if she was certain of not offending his taste. So she put on her slate-grey velvet skirt, and a claret-coloured Pucci shirt of crêpe-de-chine. She did her hair up in a knot with the side pieces softly drooping to frame her face; she wore the claret-coloured nail varnish and lipstick to match the shirt, and some very sophisticated smoky-grey mascara with a paler grey eye-shadow; and with the final addition of her plain gold torc and a chunky gold bracelet, she was ready.

A final glance in her bedroom mirror assured her that she looked elegant and mature – the kind of woman who would inspire confidence in a man like Bruno – and then she picked up the jacket that matched the skirt and her handbag and ran downstairs, and a few moments later she was roaring along the M4 extension in her car and humming to herself with happiness. After all, there was nothing like a career to take a person's mind off the complications of love, requited or unrequited.

Simon opened the door to her, and greeted her with a friendly smile.

'Hello, Celia. Come on in. You look marvellous.'

'Thanks,' she said. He led her through to the drawing-room. His flat was the mirror-image of the one she had been in on Saturday night, an elegant Edwardian structure with high ceilings, moulded plaster, large sash-windows, marble fireplaces and – nice relic of more opulent times – service bells in each room which rang through to a dolls-eye indicator in the huge kitchen. Simon's taste seemed fairly severe – the walls and ceilings were all plain white distemper, and there were few pictures or ornaments; but the carpets and curtains were of plain, rich colours – deep-blue, moss-green, burgundy – which gave a warm and solid comfort to the rooms; this was matched by the furniture, which was of the men's club type, all dark leather and polished wood.

'Welcome to the humble abode,' Simon said with a wry face that Celia assumed was meant to conceal pride in his surroundings.

'It's beautiful,' she said. 'Like the library of some terribly exclusive Piccadilly club.'

Simon beamed – she must have said the right thing. 'How perceptive you are,' he said. 'That was where I got the chairs and sofa from. Would you like some coffee?'

'Not just now, thanks – I think I'll wait until the director gets here. What time is he due? I'm dying to meet him. I never thought in all those months I toiled away at the Beeb that I'd ever meet Walter Bruno face to face.'

'He's coming at half-past ten,' Simon said. 'Are you nervous? Don't be too overawed – he is a man, as other men are. Did you read the script through? Of course you did, silly question. What did you think of it?'

Celia turned her mouth down, and Simon laughed.

'I know what you mean. A little too saccharine?'

'Slip me a dose of quinine to take the taste away,' Celia said.

'Mm, but translated into visual terms – '

'Oh yes, I agree – I think it has a lot of potential, but it would have to be very carefully done to avoid bathos.'

'That was why I wanted Bruno to do it. Do you remember *Les Enfants Etourdis*? That subtle understatement – '

'Oh yes, I thought it terribly effective,' Celia said. 'It actually made me cry at the end where – '

'Yes, me too,' Simon said eagerly. 'Do you know the old Japanese saying in support of understatement? It goes something like "Speak only of the wound, for the pain will speak of itself".'

'That's very good. But, Simon, all the same, you have to think of money. Much as I hate to bring the nasty stuff into a conversation on such a high level, *Les Enfants* drew a very limited audience even in its own country – '

'Yes, I know, but this script is in a quite different vein. I thought with a bit of judicious handling from Bruno and us, we could play both ends of the market with this one, and them as couldn't see the significance could still enjoy the story.'

'In the same way that you did with *Death of a Patriot*?'

'Ah, you noticed the significance in that, did you?' Simon smiled at her. She grinned back.

'Fair reeked of symbolism, it did, guv.'

'Well I'm glad someone noticed. The critics all but called it a heart-warming tale of love and courage.'

'Well, so it was,' Celia said cheerfully. 'You speak as if you've an aversion to earning money. Don't forget your backers.'

'God bless 'em,' Simon said solemnly. 'As if I ever could. Like the poor, them I have always with me. Are you sure you wouldn't like some coffee?'

'Well, since you press me – '

'Come into the kitchen with me, then, and talk to me while I make it.'

Celia preceded him from the room, and when she reached the kitchen and turned to look at him, she saw Simon was looking at her with a quizzical expression.

'What's up?' she asked.

'I was just wondering how you knew the way to my kitchen, despite the fact that you've never been here before. You *haven't* ever been here before, have you? I wouldn't like to think my memory was failing me *that* badly.'

'No, don't worry, you haven't missed anything,' Celia said, smiling at the thought. 'It was just that I went to a party on Saturday night which, by a strange coincidence, happened to be held at a flat just across the road from here, and it was identical in layout, except, of course, back to front.'

'Whose flat was that, then?'

'Toby Llewellyn's.'

'My dear, you do move in exalted circles! How do you come to know Toby?'

'I don't,' Celia said. 'I was taken along by a friend who knows her professionally. Do you know her?'

'Oh yes,' Simon said non-committally. Celia suddenly remembered.

'Oh, I saw someone there you *would* know – your friend Christopher Shalako.'

Until she said it, she had no idea of looking for a reaction in Simon, but when he looked a little uncomfortable and removed his gaze from her she suddenly wondered if there was anything – any grain of truth in the story. She could not believe he was homosexual, though she had heard that sometimes there is a touch of it in the most heterosexual-seeming people.

'Ah, yes, Christopher,' he said vaguely, and then changed the subject. 'We have to lunch Bruno, you know, and I was wondering whether to have something here or take him out – what do you think?'

'I don't really know,' Celia said, falling in with him. 'I suppose it depends on how much work we still have to do.' They discussed the lunch problem, and the slight awkwardness of the moment passed.

Walter Bruno arrived exactly on time, and at once seemed to fill

37

the flat with his vitality. He was over sixty, and his hair was white, but his elegant figure was as upright and, apparently, as supple as a young man's; he had a sun tan even more expensive than Toby's and Boris's, which contrasted wonderfully with his white hair and blue eyes; and he exuded such a positive air of health and vigour that Celia caught herself thinking of the old Kruschen Salts advert. He shook Simon's hand, and bowed to Celia – the kind of gesture that would only look right from a man of his standing – and said,

'I am delighted to meet you, delighted. Please at once to call me Walter – ' he pronounced it the German way, with a 'v' sound at the beginning – 'because we shall be working together so much, and "Mr Bruno" sounds so much like a nice toy bear in a puppet show, so please, it is Walter, yes?'

'Yes,' was all Celia managed to get in before, with a flashing white smile, he was off again. He accepted coffee, and the three of them took their seats in the drawing-room and got straight down to business. Much of the initial talking was done between Simon and Walter, but Celia by no means felt like a cypher, particularly as Simon always said 'we' instead of 'I', and often referred to her for confirmation of the various points he was putting up.

'The script is terrible, terrible,' Walter said in his large way, shaking his head as if over some dreadful catastrophe, 'but we can make something of it, with hard work, lots of hard work. Is the author to do the rewriting?'

'Yes, he's agreed to it, though most of it I think will be omission rather than change, so it shouldn't prove too big a problem. We felt it certainly had potential – '

'Yes, yes, of course, I agree with you. Otherwise I would not have accepted your offer, Simon, despite the friendship I feel for you, but we shall make a good film of this bad script, we three, yes?' He smiled round, gathering them both in. *Professional charm*, Celia thought to herself, but she did not object to it. It was a way of getting on with people, and getting on with people was very important in his business.

'Now, as to the schedule,' Walter went on, 'I can be with you from the beginning of May. I assume you will be doing the location work first, yes?'

'Yes, we thought so,' Simon said, though in fact he had not discussed this point with Celia. 'If we can do the shooting in

Greece first, we may be able to get it done before the weather gets too hot, and then the rest of the location work in England when the weather is most settled.'

'But – ' Celia began in protest. She couldn't believe that Simon hadn't seen the problem. They both turned to her politely. 'But you can't do the hunting scenes until winter,' she said. A large part of the action took place on the hunting field. Both men still looked at her uncomprehendingly. They hadn't thought of it, that was obvious. She smiled inwardly, and explained. 'Hunting takes place only in winter, when the trees are bare. You can't film hunting scenes in the summer. Even if you could find a way of stripping the trees, the horses wouldn't steam, and their breath wouldn't smoke. And all the colours would be wrong.'

'Yes, of course, of course. This is true,' Walter said, visualizing it. 'This is a very good point.'

'I hadn't thought of it,' Simon said, 'but it's so obvious. Thank you, Celia. Of course, you're right. We'll have to wait at least until October, maybe November. How will that tie in with your schedule, Walter?'

He shrugged. 'We shall see. If we manage things well, it should be no more than, say, two weeks' shooting. I can fit this in with other matters if we have tied everything else up.'

'Good. That's settled then.' Simon went on to other points. They talked fast, and to the point, and got through much more than Celia would have expected, and when it came to lunch time, the exalted Walter Bruno waved aside the idea of a restaurant lunch and suggested that bread and cheese where they were would save time.

'We can then continue to talk while we eat,' he said. 'In my life I have found that there are not enough hours in the day to spare any of them for doing only one thing at once.'

Simon laughed. 'I don't think I can entirely subscribe to that. But we shall eat here if that will satisfy you. I can do better than bread and cheese – I have a number of things laid in for a cold collation. If you would like to carry on talking with Celia, I'll go and get things ready.'

Celia glanced up, wondering if she should offer to help, and Simon caught her eye and shook his head slightly, smiling. Refreshing again, she thought, not to be equated with a catering machine because she was female; in her own book of etiquette, the host should supply the food and drink without expecting the guests to help, but so often other people did not agree with her. Simon did not take long. In fifteen minutes he was back with an array of cold meats, cheeses, pâtés and bread, with fresh fruit for a dessert and a bottle of chilled white wine to wash it down. The three of them ate and talked, and afterwards Celia thought that they could not have had a better meal if they *had* gone out – more expensive, certainly, and more pretentious, possibly, but not better.

After lunch they got down to the subject of casting. It was the job of the producer to cast the extras, and sometimes the minor roles, but the director had the say in the casting of the major roles, although, of course, he usually discussed his ideas with the producer.

'For the heroine, for – ' Walter checked the script – 'Madeleine, I want somebody entirely fresh and new. There is a kind of innocence in her, an unselfconscious approach to life, that requires a face no one knows, a fresh face. It will mean a lot of auditioning, I know – ' he spread his hands regretfully 'but . . .' He let the sentence hang.

'Once we have an idea of exactly what you want, we can do the screening-auditions first,' Simon suggested. Walter nodded.

'I think so. And then, for the hero, for Charles – I don't like that name, by the way, *Charles*, I don't like it.' He screwed his face up peevishly. 'It sounds like the child in the nursery who won't eat his greens. No, it must be changed. But for now, for Charles, I know exactly who I want. Not an obvious choice, but once you have thought about it, you will see why I think so. It is the young man who played Wellington in *Eve of Waterloo* – what is this his name is – '

Walter screwed up his face in thought. *Inevitable*, Celia thought calmly. *Hey ho – hear a name and within the day –*

'Maxwell Prior,' she said. Walter's face lit up.

'That is the name. Yes, yes, that is the young man I mean. Maxwell Prior.' He looked from Celia to Simon and back again with an anticipatory smile. 'Now then – what do you think?'

FOUR

Now the work really began in earnest. The shabby office in St Martin's Lane became the centre of operations, and the telephone rang almost continuously, when it could find the time between making calls out. Bill answered it with one hand, while with the other he tended the Xerox machine as it stuttered through the endless copies which were needed of the script. Some of these would be sent to the agents of actors they wanted to take part in the film, and to other agents who usually supplied Simon with extras; others would be sent to heads of such 'service' departments as Costume and Wardrobe, so that they would have time to study the characters and, if necessary, mug up on the historical period. It was necessary that they should know what people looked like and what people wore.

One of Simon's first jobs was to telephone Maxwell Prior's agent to sound him out on the chances of Prior being free for the part. The agent was not enthusiastic.

'He's free all right,' he said, but in such a doubtful tone of voice Simon might have supposed the police were at that moment knocking on Prior's door with a hot warrant in each hand. 'Oh yes, he's *free*, but what on earth is this you're sending me, Simon? *An Edwardian spy story?* Simon, you're an old friend, to an old friend I wouldn't be rude, but I have to tell you Simon that it stinks. The idea stinks. Who on earth could have written such a thing? And besides, Maxie just did a costume bit for *Auntie*; more costumes he doesn't need. I know for a fact, Simon, and I wouldn't tell you this, only you're an old friend, but I know for a fact that Maxie doesn't like to do costume drama, he doesn't want to do any more costume drama, at least not this year.'

Simon listened patiently, and then said, 'It isn't as if it's Elizabethan, Phil – it's only Edwardian. That's practically modern dress, as far as the men go. And Edwardian is very popular at the moment. Why don't you just see what he thinks? Walter Bruno is directing and he thinks it will be really great, only he very badly wants Max Prior, so I have to ask.'

41

'Of course I'll ask him, Simon, what do you think? Send me a copy of the script and I'll do what I can to persuade him, but only because you're a friend. And if he decides he can do without an old man nagging him to take parts he doesn't like – ' Simon could hear the shrug at the other end.

'Thanks, Phil. I'll leave it to you.'

Simon told Celia about the conversation afterwards, adding, 'I know Phil pretty well, when he's play-acting and when he's not. I think this time he really thinks Prior might turn it down.'

'I wouldn't be too sorry if he did, from a purely personal point of view,' Celia said.

'Why's that?'

'I met Maxwell Prior at a party.'

'You didn't tell me,' Simon smiled. 'What exalted circles you BBC people move in.'

'Don't be sarcastic,' Celia said.

'Anyway, what did you think of Prior? Didn't like him?' Simon hazarded. Celia made a face. 'Oh. Didn't like him,' he concluded. 'Well, despite that, I hope he accepts, and if he does you'll have to mask your feelings, bottle yourself up, and be noble.'

'Of course I will. Noble is the word that describes me, all right,' Celia said.

Auditioning started for the extras, and for the female lead, the former being dealt with by Celia and the latter by Simon. For the extras they wanted men with moustaches for preference, for it made Make-up's job considerably easier not to have to fix face-hair, but it seemed that every extra in London at that season had a full set or nothing. Celia felt she ought to have a recording made of the questions she had to put every time: 'Are you willing to shave off the beard?' or 'How do you feel about growing a moustache?' The worst problem would not be theirs, however. Edwardian hair was worn fairly full; but Celia had had experience of filming a wartime story, and the problem was to persuade the modern young man to get his hair cut short back and sides.

When they weren't auditioning, Celia and Simon were going through the script together, word for word, scene by scene. It got so that they knew it back-to-front and upside-down, and Celia, when she fell into bed exhausted at night, would find herself repeating the dialogue endlessly in her dreams. They met the author briefly, and found him so nervous and irritable, such an unpleasant mixture of arrogance and insecurity that afterwards Simon suggested privately to Celia that they did as much of the rewriting themselves as possible.

'He'll never notice, I'm sure,' Simon said.

'I thought writers knew every syllable of their own stuff,' Celia said.

'Anyone who could write anything as bad as that mustn't have paid it much attention in the first place,' Simon said firmly. 'Anyway, he'll be easy enough to bully. We're paying him for the wretched thing after all.'

Celia had to smile. 'The way we talk about this script, anyone would be forgiven for wondering why we're bothering with it.'

One of Celia's more arduous tasks was the drawing up of schedules, great sheets of columned paper on which the presence or absence of any character in any scene could be traced. There were schedules for the stars, for the extras, and for the service departments. Everything had to be mapped out, from the where abouts of the leading couple to the presence on a certain table at a certain moment of a musical box that would actually play *Au Clair de la Lune* when wound up. Props like that that actually worked were called 'practicals' and everyone in Celia's position had tales to tell of dreadful moments in filming when, for instance, a fountain-pen snatched up by the hero refused to write. It was the stage manager's job to see that practicals worked when they were supposed to, but the stage manager worked off schedules laid down by the producer, so the ultimate responsibility was Celia's.

One morning when Celia and Bill were alone at the office, Maxwell Prior's agent rang with the news that he had turned down the part. Bill put him through to Celia.

'I'm sorry I can't oblige, specially since Simon's an old friend, but Maxie says no costumes,' Phil said.

'Is that the only reason?' Celia asked. 'What did he think of the play as a whole?'

'The part I think he quite liked. He *did* say to me what a pity they set it in Edwardian times, as if the same thing in modern dress he would not say no to. But he said to me, "Phil," he said, "another six months of horsehair whiskers and tight trousers I don't need." So, I'm sorry, but it's no.'

Celia phoned the bad news straight through to Simon, who was at his flat with Walter.

'I was afraid of that,' Simon said. 'I didn't think Phil was putting it on. Oh well, it's back to the drawing-board, I suppose.'

Half an hour later he rang back.

'Walter wants you to try and persuade Prior to take the part,' Simon said, with uncharacteristic bluntness.

'Me?' Celia said in amazement. 'Why on earth me?'

'You've met him,' Simon said. 'Walter thinks you might succeed on a personal level where business tactics fail. He's quite desperate to have Prior for the part, so I suppose he's willing to try anything.'

'*He*'s willing to try?' Celia snorted.

'All right, but what will it cost you to have a go?' Simon cajoled.

'Simon, I met him and didn't like him Why on earth should he accept the part from me when he wouldn't accept it from his agent?'

'You're prettier than Phil.'

'Don't be funny. He didn't even like me. He wouldn't even remember me.'

'If he didn't remember you, it wouldn't matter if he didn't like you the first time, would it?' Simon said. 'But in any case, he'll both remember you and like you. Who could do otherwise?'

'This flattery doesn't convince me of anything except that you're clutching at straws,' Celia said severely.

'You're right,' Simon admitted. 'I don't know why you should succeed either, but Walter very much wants you to try, and I can't see that it can do any harm, so won't you, Celia, please? Just try?'

Celia sighed. 'Oh all right. What do you want me to do?'

'Can you get to meet him socially in the next couple of days? Your friends whose party you met at – could they arrange a chance meeting do you think?'

'I've no idea. I'll find out. I don't even know if he lives in London.'

'He does – somewhere in Kew I believe. Practically on your doorstep.'

'How convenient. All right, and if I can get to meet him?'

'Make friends with him and then ask him as a favour to take

on the part,' Simon suggested simply. Celia thought for a long moment.

'It sounds suspiciously like white-slaving. I'll do what sweet-talk can do, but no more, you understand that, Simon.'

Simon sounded shocked. 'Celia, whatever can you mean? I wouldn't want you to – I wouldn't dream of – '

'I bloody well hope not,' Celia said. 'All right – I'll let you know. Anything else while you're on?'

'No, nothing. Thanks, Celia. Don't worry too much if it doesn't come off.'

Celia hung up, thinking that things coming off was precisely what she was worrying about.

'You want to meet Max Prior?' Eva said. 'Cely, why on earth?'

'Never mind,' Celia said patiently. 'Can you fix it?'

'Max Prior,' Eva wondered aloud again. 'I can't imagine – on the strength of that one meeting – Celia, you can't possibly be going to fall in love with him, not straight after Dick the Prick? Not two rotters in one year?'

'No, Eva, don't be silly. Of course I'm not. Please, credit me with a little sense.'

'I wish I could. I wish I could suppose – wait a minute! I've got it! Are you at last going to take my advice and spread your wings a bit? Is El Prior the chosen candidate for the Spare Time Screw Award? I say, Celia, when you do a thing you don't do it by halves, do you?'

'I never was one to mince my bones,' Celia said modestly. It would not do for Eva to think this was all in the line of business. She might help Celia with her love life, but she would not lift a finger to help her to snare an actor for a part. So like Brer Fox she laid low and said nuffin.

'All right, sweetheart, I'll see what I can do. Toby owes me a favour. I'll give her a ring, and phone you back.'

Celia thanked her and rang off, already feeling a little grubbier than before.

Eva rang back a couple of hours later.

'All right, it's all on, but it has to be tonight. Can you make it?'

'I have to make it,' Celia said. 'What's the score?'

'He lives at Strand-on-the-Green, and there's a pub there called The London Barge where he drinks when he drinks. Toby's going to meet him there tonight around nine, and if you stroll in casually, as if you're just coming in for a drink on your own, Toby will call you over to join them. Okay?'

'Yes, fine. The London Barge at nine o'clock. Thanks Eva.'

'That's all right. For you, for such a good cause – but I've used up my credit with Toby now, so you'd better get his trousers off tonight or not at all. Go in there with your guns blazing, kid. Only one of youse is coming out of there alive.'

Celia was about to protest that it was nothing like that, and stopped herself in time. 'Okay, Butch,' she drawled back. 'You cover m'rear.'

'What d'you think I am?' Eva snorted. 'All right, darling, tell me all about it tomorrow – or as much as I need to fire my imagination. Have fun!'

Yeah, Celia thought, hanging up again. It's a dirty business, show business. But the show must go on, and the trousers must come off. Or something.

When Celia strolled into The London Barge that evening at nine o'clock she already knew it was going to be a failure of an evening. I'm just not cut out for intrigue, she thought. Several pairs of eyes turned to her enquiringly as she walked in, and she felt that she did not look convincingly like someone who went to pubs alone for a drink just on the spur of the moment. She had dressed casually in plum-coloured cord trousers and a yellow silk shirt and had her hair caught back with two yellow, plastic butterfly slides, but she still looked as if she'd come to meet somebody, which of course she had.

Keeping her eyes to herself she went up to the bar and after a long wait got herself served with a gin and tonic, and then she turned away from the bar and cast her eyes about casually as if she was looking for somewhere to sit. Toby and Prior were over in the corner where it was dark enough for Prior not to be recognized too easily, and Toby did not seem to have spotted her yet. She was leaning towards Prior talking eagerly and seriously. Celia wondered suddenly if Eva had misunderstood, and if she would be breaking into a tête-à-tête if she went over. Still, she couldn't feel more foolish than she did already. She moved slowly towards them, still pretending to be looking for a seat, and trying to avoid the eyes of the lone males who wondered if she might be looking for them.

She was within feet of them, and wondering how she could

feign not to have seen them for a second longer, when Toby looked up, gave a small start, and then smiled and waved a hand.

'Celia!' she called, as if Celia was her dearest and longest-lost friend. 'What are you doing here? Come and join us! You know Max, don't you?'

Celia smiled and sat down gratefully in the empty chair which made a third round their table. She glanced at Prior. 'We have met, though I don't know if he'd remember.'

His face was utterly expressionless as he looked at her, but when she said that he answered quite sharply, 'I remember all right. Why shouldn't I?'

Celia turned hastily to Toby. 'I'm interrupting, aren't I? I don't want to – '

'Nonsense, darling, of course not,' Toby said, and to Celia's surprise she looked a little put-out at the suggestion. 'Max and I are just old friends. Are you meeting someone or something?'

Celia decided rapidly that the casual-drinker role was unplayable. 'I was, but I'm afraid they aren't coming. It was only a loose engagement.' She didn't want to give the impression she was the kind of person who got stood up. Oh dear, what a tangled web, etcetera. 'They said they might come but – it seems they haven't.'

'Perhaps you've got the wrong pub,' Prior suggested with an odd tone of voice. She looked at him. He was staring at her with a kind of grim cynicism which was not pleasant. He hadn't shaved, and his blue chin made him look dangerous; he was wearing a faded denim shirt, open at the neck, which gave his body a more heavy and burly look than its screen norm. Altogether, he might have been the hero from one of those hard-hitting London detective series like *Hazell* or *Target*.

'No,' Celia said rather feebly. 'It's the right pub.'

'Then perhaps it's the wrong night,' he suggested, equally rudely. At that moment Celia's pride revolted at her task. She began to stand up.

'Look, I'm sorry. I didn't mean to butt in. I'll go somewhere else.'

'Celia, darling, don't be silly, you aren't butting in,' Toby said, sounding anxious. 'I don't know why Max is being so cross. Why are you cross, darling? Tell Celia you don't mean it.'

Prior's eyes had not left Celia's face, but he said, 'Of course I don't mean it. I never mean anything.' He said it with such significance that Celia wondered if by some weird second sight he knew why she was there. 'Sit down, Celia. You aren't butting in. Can I get you a drink?'

'Thanks, but this will last me.'

'Answer the question. Can I get you a drink?' he said.

'No, thank you,' she answered. Her heart was in her boots now. He definitely didn't like her; she was, despite what he said, butting in on something. Maybe Toby was having an affair with him. The best thing she could do would be to drink up quickly and get out, and tell Simon in the morning that Prior was so unfriendly towards her that it was really a good thing that he wasn't going to take the part.

There was a short silence, during which they all must have felt awkward to a greater or lesser degree, and then Toby began to talk again in a high, nervous voice, about people that Celia did not know, but Prior presumably did. He did not help her out, but grunted assent now and then, his eyes on his glass and his fingers turning a beer-mat endlessly round and round. Celia glanced at him cautiously from time to time. She saw there was a small muscle ticking in his jaw, and she wondered why he was so tense. Was her presence making him nervous? Did he think she would tell Boris? But she couldn't imagine him being worried about Boris, a famous film star like Maxwell Prior.

She noticed things about him here, in the ordinary light of the pub, which she had not noticed in the heat and crush of the party, and which, of course, she hadn't noticed when he was on the screen. His eyelashes, for instance, were absurdly long, and when they drooped over his eyes as at the moment, they made him look very sad, and very young. There were one or two silver hairs in amongst the black that were somehow strangely touching, especially since his delicate black eyebrows were also sparked with silver. Somehow, one did not expect eyebrows to go grey.

There was a tiny scar like a crescent near the corner of his mouth which only showed up because of the way the light fell. When he smiled, she imagined it would be hidden by the smile-creases, and of course under make-up it wouldn't show at all. And there was this unexpected weight and power about his neck and shoulders. On the screen he always gave the impression of being very slender and light, like a young boy, but in fact he was strongly, powerfully made, extremely male. She looked from the hard curve of his neck-muscles to the subtle curve of his lips and she suddenly shivered in reaction to him. She withdrew her eyes from him a split second before he raised his to her, and though aware of his gaze on her she kept her eyes fixed on Toby and nodded as if she were listening to what Toby said.

As soon as there was a pause in Toby's rattling narrative, Celia drained her glass and stood up.

'Well, it's been nice talking to you,' she said, 'but I think I'd better be going. My friends obviously aren't coming. Thanks for inviting me over, Toby.'

'But you aren't going, surely,? Toby asked, looking surprised. 'Stay for another drink at least. Max was just going to get a round.'

'No, thanks all the same. I'd better be getting back,' Celia said, and Prior, standing up at the same time, said,

'I wasn't getting a round, actually. I'm going home to bed. I'll see you again soon, Toby – I'll give you a ring next week some time.'

Celia was a little taken aback, and glanced from him to Toby, but the latter shrugged as if to say, one way or another, what does it matter? Prior appeared to be waiting to walk out of the pub with her, and so Celia said goodbye again to Toby and left her, feeling a little guilty, with Prior following her. Outside she walked without a word to the place where she had parked her car, and then she turned to Prior and said, knowing he would refuse, 'Can I give you a lift anywhere?'

'I live a hundred yards away, up the road, but I suppose I might as well ride it as walk it.'

Oh, she thought, swallowing. Now what? She got in at her side and opened the door for him; he slid into the passenger seat and looked round him with interest.

'Is this your car?' he asked.

'Yes,' Celia said, slightly surprised. Whose car did he think she would drive?

'I like it,' he said. So what? she thought. He seemed to read her thoughts, because he said, 'My approval may not mean much to you, but my *friends* count me a connoisseur of cars. This is one of the great cars of all time. A classic.'

'That's why I bought it. I love it,' Celia said. 'Where to?'

'That way,' he indicated. 'It's a white house with a red door. On the left.'

She started the engine, turned the car, and drove slowly up the road, looking for the house. 'There,' he said in a moment, and she drew in to the kerb and stopped in front of the house he indicated. It had been literally a couple of hundred yards. She wondered what it was all about, and waited for him to get out, but he didn't. He sat in silence, staring through the windscreen as if deep in thought, while she waited impatiently. At last he sighed, and turned to her, and fixed her with his eyes.

'All right, do you want to tell me what it's all about?'

'What what's all about?' Celia said, considerably startled.

'What's going on between you and Toby? She dragged me out to the pub on some feeble pretext, and then you turned up looking as if we were the very last people you expected to see in the pub, into which you, a person who would never enter a pub alone, had come alone.' Celia said nothing. He went on, 'You asked Toby to fix it for you to meet me, didn't you? Why?' Celia still said nothing. She couldn't think of anything to say. Prior looked down at his nails, and then out of the window, and went on,

'I can hardly believe it of Toby, but I am forced to the conclusion that you asked her to introduce you to me in the hopes that I would take you to bed.'

Celia's head jerked round and she began to make an exclamation of annoyance, but he looked round at her and raised an eyebrow and silenced her.

'Look at the evidence, my dear young lady. You obviously rigged a meeting but when I was rude to you, you lost heart and gave up. When you got up to go, you didn't expect me to come with you. Therefore you must have abandoned your scheme when you saw I wasn't going to fall for your lovely eyes and pretty hair.'

'Quite a detective, aren't you?' Celia snapped. 'You're right, I did have a reason for wanting to meet you, and I wouldn't have said anything about it now, but I wouldn't like you to go off with the impression that it was for your fabulous face that I wanted to meet you.'

'It wasn't?' he said in mock-surprise.

'No,' she spat. 'It wasn't. It was purely business.'

'Oh, is that what you call it?' he said. Celia's blood pressure was rising slowly, but she saw now that she must tell all, and was cool enough to wonder if she might still wrest an advantage from the situation. She forced herself to speak in a normal voice.

'It wasn't a task that I wanted – it was rather forced on me, and when I was actually faced with you, I felt I couldn't go through with it, and I was withdrawing when you insisted on coming with me. I work for Simon Davis – Bantham Films. Walter Bruno thought I might have more chance of persuading you to take on the part in *The Athens Affair* if I made friends with you and asked you as a personal favour. I thought it was a poor scheme,and when I met you in the pub I realized it would never work. That's all there is to it.'

There was a silence. Prior had looked away from her when she began to speak, and was now studying his nails again. He looked uneasy. A little embarrassed, perhaps, at what he had said previously? No, it didn't look like embarrassment. It looked more like disappointment. Celia contemplated with awe the size of an ego which could feel disappointed at a juncture like that.

'So that's it, is it?' Prior said quietly. Then he looked up with a strange hardness in his expression. 'All right, I'll do a deal with you. You must really love your job to consider doing a thing like that, and I wouldn't want to ruin your career over something that doesn't really matter too much to me. I'd already had second thoughts about that script. I'll do it – on one condition.'

'What's that?' Celia said warily. She was not yet overjoyed. Even if the condition was reasonable, her job did not depend on her getting Maxwell Prior for the lead, and as she had already said, on a personal level she'd sooner have someone else to work with.

'That you spend the day with me tomorrow – the whole day – and do exactly as I ask you.'

Celia stared at him with surprise, and her colour rose slowly. 'I don't think I can agree to do exactly as you tell me,' she said tartly. His face twisted into an unpleasantly cynical smile.

'Oh don't worry, I haven't got any designs on your body, attractive though it may be to some. *I* wouldn't ask you to sell yourself, though apparently your boss would.' Celia's jaw dropped at this insult to Simon, but she had no time to protest, for he went on, 'No, all I want is your company – your willing, good-humoured company. It'll be no good if you sulk or act hostilely towards me. I want you to pretend, at least, that we are friends.'

Celia considered. She seemed to have nothing to lose, if that were the case. And if it was not, she could always back out. 'All right,' she shrugged. 'What do you want me to do?'

'Have you ever tried wind-surfing?' he asked abruptly.

'No,' she said.

'We're going wind-surfing,' he said. 'You'd better wear jeans or something like that. And bring a swimming-costume – you have *got* a swimming-costume, I suppose – and I don't mean a bikini?'

'Yes,' she said. 'But it's far too cold to be doing anything like that at this time of year.'

He grinned. 'Not where we're going,' he said. He felt in the pocket of his shirt, and brought out an envelope and a stub of a pencil. 'Here,' he said, 'write your address on the back of this. And your phone number in case. I'll call for you at a quarter to eight tomorrow morning, and you'd better be ready because we want to get to the airport before the traffic gets too heavy.'

'The airport?' Celia said.

'Lydd,' he said. 'Don't worry, I'll have you home before your DB turns into a pumpkin. We do this my way, that's the bargain. Write your address.'

Celia obeyed, and handed the envelope back to him, and without further ado he got out of the car, saying as he banged the door shut, 'A quarter to eight tomorrow. Be ready. Don't forget the swimming-costume.'

He crossed the pavement to the house, but as Celia was leaning to turn on the ignition again, he came back and tapped on the window. She ran it down, and he poked his head in.

'What's your name, apart from Celia?' he asked.

'Bancroft,' she said.

'Celia Bancroft.' He tried it over. 'Cor, bloody 'ell.' And he was gone, this time for good.

FIVE

Celia telephoned Simon at home as soon as she got in, to tell him of the latest development. Simon seemed very doubtful about the whole thing.

'I don't like it,' he said. 'It sounds odd. I wonder what he can be up to? Look, Celia, I think you should call it off. We'll get someone else to play the part, and Walter will just have to get used to the idea. I don't want you doing something you don't like.'

A bit late for that sort of scruple, Celia thought to herself, and remembered Prior's words – 'I don't want you to sell yourself...' She said, 'I won't do anything I don't like. He says he just wants my company, and I think I'm a big enough girl by now to see that's all he gets. If it looks like being anything else I'll be off like a scalded cat, don't you worry.'

'I wasn't even thinking of that,' Simon said. 'I wouldn't want you even to bear his company if it was blackmail on his part.'

'It's a kind of blackmail, I suppose,' Celia admitted, 'but I think I might as well go through with it, now I've got this far. If you can manage without me tomorrow, of course.'

'Oh, yes, we can manage all right. I'm just worried about you, that's all.'

'Don't worry. I'll be all right. I'll give you a ring tomorrow night if I get back in time, and let you know how I got on.'

'Yes, do, and Celia, be careful – '

'Don't worry,' she said again. 'Anyway, I've always wanted to try wind-surfing.' And she hung up, before he could ask her how they could wind-surf at this time of year. Let him sweat that one out, she thought. Feeling jaded, she bathed and went to bed, but once there she lay awake for a long time wondering what would happen the next day, where they would go, and even more, what he was up to. What did he want her company for? The simplest explanation, that he merely fancied her, she had to reject, since it would have been so much easier all round for him to simply admit it, if that were the case. But if he didn't, why was he 'blackmailing' her into spending the day with him? Was he out to get his revenge on her for not being nice to him at the party? Yet that seemed so unreasonable, such a lot of trouble to go to for such a small thing.

She fell asleep at last, no more satisfied in her head as to his motives than as to their probable destination.

Prior was punctual the next morning, blowing a fanfare on his car horn that had her scooting to the window worrying about the neighbours. Looking down, Celia saw him just getting out of a silver-grey XJ Jaguar, and as soon as she saw it she decided that was exactly the car she would have expected him to drive. Fearing another salvo on the doorbell, she ran downstairs and let him in.

'Good morning. Are you ready?' he asked briskly.

'Yes. Come in for a minute, while I pick up my bag and things.' Some devil made her turn back with an affected simper. 'I hope I'm correctly dressed for you. I haven't got a wind-surfing outfit as such – '

'You look all right,' he said curtly. 'Hurry up.'

Ooh you are masterful, she mouthed to herself as she ran back upstairs. She had put on her Falmers jeans, which had worn to an even, soft, faded blue, and an almost transparent cheese-cloth shirt over her red and white spotted bikini. Her hair was held back from her face with a red and white cotton scarf folded into a band, and her sunglasses were balanced on top. Upstairs she collected her swimming-costume and cap and towel, grabbed her saddle-stitched shoulder-bag that matched her sandals, and her bright red oiled-silk bomber jacket, and ran down again with a show of not wanting to keep him waiting. He noticed.

'All right, relax, you can stop play-acting.'

'Sorry,' she said demurely. 'I forgot that was your department.'

He feigned to ignore that remark. 'Got your costume?'

'Yes. A plain, navy, Olympic-style racing costume. All right?'

'And a cap, I see. You must be a swimmer to own gear like that. I'm glad. Most women seem to think ankle-deep is as far as they can go in the water without dissolving.'

'Thank you for those few kind words, Mr Prior,' Celia said, 'but I must warn you that if you are going to make foolish sexist generalizations like that all day, I shall very likely feel constrained to weight your feet with my handbag and drown you.'

Suddenly he laughed, lighting up his face and showing Celia for the first time the charm that had made him a pin-up for thousands of girls all over the world. 'Fair enough,' he said. 'We must call a truce. I want this to be a pleasant day, and our agreement is that we must appear to be friends, so let's start now.' He held out his hand to her, and she shook it, and smiled. 'That's better,' he said. 'And since we have to be friends, it would seem more natural if you called me Max. And I'll call you Celia.'

'Right. Shall we go, then? Oh – do I need a passport?'

'You might as well bring it, if you have an up-to-date one,' he said. 'Oh, but of course you would, being a producer's assistant.'

'It's already in my bag,' she said, and with a nod of approval he led the way out. 'I like your car,' she said as she stood beside it, waiting to be let in. From the upholstery and the dashboard trim, she could see it was not new, although it was in immaculate condition. 'It reminds me of mine.'

He glanced back down the road at her own navy-blue DB and smiled. 'I know what you mean. Actually, I should imagine they are about the same age as each other. Somehow a new, modern car doesn't have the same feeling about it. What I'd really like is a nineteen-fifties' Humber or Riley – one of those where you sit so high up it's almost like driving a coach.'

'And the doors open the other way, so that you can get in without killing yourself,' she said.

'And they have a good wide running-board for carrying dead sheep on,' he finished. He got in and opened her door from inside, and she slid in beside him to the pleasant smell of well-kept leather. There was an interesting array of dials and switches on the dashboard which made it look like the cockpit of a plane.

'Very impressive,' she said, nodding towards them. He glanced and smiled.

'The clever part is remembering what they all are. It doesn't impress one's companion when you casually flick on the windscreen-wipers and get a lighted cigarette flying at you.'

'I suppose,' Celia began – she was about to say, 'I suppose impressing your companion is a big thing in your life', but she remembered in time that she was contracted to be friendly, and so she changed it, leaning forward and touching a switch, to 'I suppose this is the windscreen-wipers?'

He glanced. 'No, that's the fuel-tank switch. There are two of them, and when you're on a long journey, travelling fast, you have to switch from one tank to the other at intervals so as to use the fuel evenly and keep the car's balance right.'

'Oh,' she said. 'I'm impressed.' He glanced at her doubtfully as he turned the car on to the main road. 'Talking of long journeys,' she went on, 'where are we going?'

He glanced at her again, as if wondering whether, or how much, to tell her. 'Southern Spain,' he said. 'Private plane. You'll see.'

Whatever it was they were doing, it was obvious that Max, as she must learn to call him, had done it before. After a hair-raisingly fast drive to the airport, he conducted Celia at a brisk walk to a small lounge which they entered through a door marked 'Private – Staff Only' where two people were waiting for them. To Celia's surprise she recognized them both. One was Christopher Shalako; the other was the stunningly beautiful, red-headed film star, sex-symbol of half the male population of the world, Rain Bacchus.

'Oh there you are!' the lady flung at Max in tones of dramatic exasperation. 'You're late again, you're always late. I'm sick of waiting for you every time we decide to do anything. And who's *that*, for God's sake?' She didn't quite point at Celia with a quivering finger, but her tone of voice was that in which one would apostrophize something brown and sticky on the carpet.

'*That*,' Max said, flinging her tone of voice back at her, 'is my *very good* friend, Celia Bancroft. Celia, allow me to introduce our hostess for the day, Rain Bacchus, better known to many as the Bust of British – '

'Can it, Charlie,' Rain said sharply. 'If you're going to start that – '

'Perish the thought, darling. I withdraw it unreservedly,' Max said quickly. 'And this languid creature you probably know,' he went on, turning to Christopher Shalako, who, to Celia's surprise, stood up and offered her his hand quite politely saying,

'Celia Bancroft. It rings a bell. I'm sure I've met you somewhere. Your face seems familiar.'

'I'll bet it does,' Rain Bacchus muttered not quite inaudibly.

'Are you an actor?' Shalako went on to Celia, still holding her hand. His was limp and slightly moist, and Celia had to control an urge to throw it away. It felt like a dead fish.

'No,' she said. 'I was at Toby Llewellyn's party the other week. Maybe you saw me there.'

He released her hand and snapped his fingers, the kind of gesture that only actors can make successfully.

'Pink pyjamas,' he said. 'I knew I knew your face.'

'As I remember the pyjamas,' Max said, 'it wasn't her face you'd have been looking at.'

'But how do you come to know my stepmother?' Shalako went on. 'If you aren't an actor – '

'Celia is a producer,' Max said for her. Rain's eyebrows climbed her forehead.

'How about that for a reversal of roles?' she said nastily. 'It used to be poor actresses going to bed with directors in the good old days.'

'*Autres jours*, darling,' Max responded smoothly. 'I think you yourself said the *dernier mot* on that subject, so one has to try something new.'

'You can be a real bitch when you try, Charlie,' Rain said savagely, and Christopher Shalako put his arm round her and said mildly to Max,

'All right, now you've got her frothing, can we have an armistice? You're going to make me very tired if you're going to keep this up all day.'

'Willingly,' Max said. 'And talking about all day, hadn't we better make a move?' He moved to Celia's side and put an arm round her shoulders. She flinched in surprise and then, remembering the bargain, controlled herself. 'We don't want to miss the tide, do we?' And with that he ushered Celia towards the door, and in going out of it she managed to slip his, albeit casual, embrace in a fairly natural way.

Rain and Christopher led the way across the tarmac to a small plane which was quietly revving its engines while waiting for them. Inside it turned out to be a six-seater, and was very fetchingly trimmed out in two shades of blue, with carpet on the floor and curtains at the window. Rain poked her head into the cockpit and addressed the pilot rapidly in what Celia assumed, from the lisp, to be Spanish, and then returned to the body of the craft to direct them tersely to 'strap up'.

'Is this her own plane?' Celia asked Max, who was sitting beside her, in an undertone.

'It is,' he told her. 'It's a gift from her latest husband, who is a Spanish millionaire. We are going to his villa, which has a private landing-strip and a private beach and every damn thing that *ouvres* and *fermes*, as the French say. Mr Rain is away, hence the presence of your friend and mine, Christopher Shalako, the boneless wonder. He can do it in positions most people only dream of. Rain's great talent in life is achieving in reality those things most people only dream of. It will probably kill her in the end.'

'Talking about me, darling?' Rain called across from her seat on the other side of the plane.

'Of course, darling. Wouldn't you be cross if I wasn't?'

'Yes, darling, I would, but didn't your best friend ever tell you that you should never talk to one girlfriend about another? Poor little Miss Bancroft will be *so* upset.'

'Miss Bancroft is neither poor nor little, and, I strongly suspect, doesn't give a bugger for you or anything you say, so I think you're wasting your time trying to upset her.'

'Trying to upset her, Charlie? Perish the thought. I'll be as nice as pie to her all day, you just see if I won't.'

The roar of the engines prevented any more of this light banter, for which Celia was grateful. It was true that in the long term she didn't care what Rain Bacchus thought or said about her, but on the other hand it wasn't pleasant to be the continuous butt of such verbal small-arms fire. The plane throttled up, they were pressed back into their seats by the thrust of the forward acceleration, and then the light craft skipped into the air; a few minutes later they were unbuckling their seat-belts while Rain lit herself a black Sobranie cigarette and directed Christopher to open a bottle of champagne.

'Pink,' she added. 'I've got four bottles on ice. I wish I could persuade Carlos to buy magnums, but he thinks they're wasteful – so absurd, when it's as cheap as water in Spain. Hurry up, Chris, I want to get a bottle inside me as soon as possible. I'm terrified of flying. I can only face it when I'm good and drunk.'

Celia noted that though she said this in a bantering tone, she did look slightly green, and there was a fine dew of sweat on her upper lip that could not be accounted for by the cool spring weather. She felt a sudden pity for the other woman. It must be a terrible disability for someone in her line of business to be afraid of flying. Soon there was the pleasant sound of the champagne cork popping, and Chris was handing her a tall goblet filled with the happiest drink in the world. Celia had never had pink champagne before. It didn't seem to taste any different, but the colour certainly gave one a festive feeling.

The first bottle was quickly emptied and the second opened, and the party began to relax. Celia would have liked to look out of the window, for she had never flown in a small plane before, and the view was quite different from that from an airliner; but, though at first the other three tended to talk about people she didn't know, or had only heard of as famous names, the conversation soon grew more lively and general, and by the time they were halfway down the second bottle, Rain was relaxed enough to get up and dance the *pas de deux* she had learned for her last film, in which she played a ballerina and Chris, appropriately, played the lead dancer.

'It all looks terribly clever,' Rain said over her shoulder as they moved in the confined space, 'but in fact it's a series of – what are they called, Chris?'

'Attitudes,' he said, supporting her by one hand and waist. 'Fixed positions. Mind you, I will say for old Rain, she's very fit and supple for her age. I don't know any other actresses who would have picked them up so easily. But all we do, you see, is the series of attitudes, and the camera cuts from one to the other so that you never see us actually taking them up.'

'The distance work was done by a girl from the Royal Ballet,' Rain said. She was panting slightly from the exertion, but then she had drunk rather a lot of champagne.

'With Chris? Or with another dancer?' Max asked. Chris looked offended.

'With me, of course. Do you mind? I'm not too old to do my own dancing yet, you know.'

'I saw you dancing at Toby's party,' Celia said, and immediately wished she hadn't, because it drew attention to her.

'Did you?' Chris said eagerly. 'We were only mucking about. Here, you come and try this one – it's easy, isn't it, Rain?'

'Easy,' Rain panted, dropping her leg to the floor and standing back from Chris with a mock bow. 'Come on, have a try.'

'I couldn't,' Celia said. 'Not in these jeans. They're too tight.'

'Take 'em off, then,' Max suggested blandly. 'I don't mind.'

'Later, Charlie, later,' Rain said. 'Give the girl a chance to get her breath.'

'On the beach, then,' Chris said, not swerving from the main

59

point. 'We'll do it on the beach. I'll show you. You look quite fit.'

'I try to keep fit,' Celia said, 'though sometimes it's hard to get it in with work. But I fence and play squash, and swim, and ride when I can get into the country.'

'I'm impressed,' Max said. 'Look at me being impressed. What an active girl you are.'

'You mean you didn't know that, Charlie?' Rain asked. 'I thought she was a *very old* friend? Or did you mean she was simply well-preserved?'

Max put his arm round Celia again. By this time she was getting tolerably used to it. 'She is an old friend. But there are some things we haven't got round to doing together.'

'Not bloody many, I'll bet,' Rain said, but she was mellow enough now not to mean it spitefully, and Celia guessed that she was simply trying to be witty. She and Chris sat down again, the glasses were refilled, and the conversation passed on to films and anecdotes about things each of them had done during filming sessions. Some of them were very funny, and all of the stories were presented with professional skill, and Celia could have listened quite happily to them all day. It being the nature of actors to talk about themselves, she did listen to them all the rest of the journey; and before she could have thought it possible, they had arrived, and were strapping themselves in for the landing.

The plane had been air-conditioned. That fact became apparent to Celia only when she stepped out on to the concrete of the small landing-strip and the sun poured down on her. She glanced up almost in surprise, and then caught Max's eye and smiled.

'I hadn't expected it to be so hot.'

'It's around seventy, I should think. Just tolerable. It doesn't get really hot here until June.'

'Seventy feels good and hot to me after London,' Rain said. 'Chris, show everybody in, will you, and show them where they can wash. Lunch should be ready. I'll just fix up the pilot – if I don't give him a firm talking-to he'll be smashed by five o'clock and we won't get back this evening.'

Chris led the other two towards the villa, which was large and rambling and painted an ice-cream pink with faded green shutters. The air was aromatic with verbena and hot thyme and juniper, and resin from the umbrella-pines that grew beside the path that led round the house. On the other side was a veranda overlooking the sea, fifty feet below at the bottom of a series of terraced gardens and a winding, gravelled path. The veranda was overhung with bougainvillea and a long table was set on it, covered with a white cloth that made your eyes ache to look at it, and was laden with china, silver and glass.

'One thing about Carlos, he always has top-class servants,' Chris sa id as they passed into the villa to be shown the bathrooms. 'They do things properly. I like that. The only point in having servants seems to me to have things done properly which you couldn't be bothered to do if you were doing them yourself. Like the table – laying it, I mean – ' he added as he left them. Celia washed her face and hands in a small modern bathroom in which everything, right down to the soap and towels and toilet-roll, were peach-coloured and matched, and then returned to the veranda feeling underdressed for the occasion. Jeans in such a mansion!

The others were gathered on the veranda, and Rain was just directing them in through another door, to where the food was spread for them to help themselves.

'I thought we'd have brunch,' Rain said casually. 'We don't want anything too heavy before going in the sea, do we?'

'Nothing too heavy' turned out to be a delicious array of hot and cold foods. In hot dishes there was scrambled eggs and crisp bacon and herb-flavoured small sausages; then there was cold fresh trout, Westphalian ham, and a rice-and-vegetable dish; there were iced Charantais melons, and fresh raspberries with a dish of thick sour-cream; *croissants* and brown rolls, and cherry jam and apricot preserve; a cona of piping-hot, fragrant coffee, and a silver ice-bucket from which protruded two more bottles of champagne.

Celia started off with scrambled eggs and bacon and raspberries, and chose coffee to drink since she had the vague feeling that swimming when you were drunk might not turn out to be a good idea. The food was delicious, and, like everyone else, she went back again and again to the table, trying little bits of everything and, despite her resolve, drinking more champagne. The talk was lively, and, though still mainly film-orientated, very interesting, and either the drink or the growing familiarity relaxed everyone so that Celia no longer felt left out. She began to think it might be very well after all to be extremely rich and live a jet-setting life of endless pleasure.

Brunch over, Rain jumped up with unexpected energy and said, 'Let's get down to the beach – the tide should be just right now, and I'm aching to be in the water. It's so hot. Chris, grab the towels will you? I put them out in the drawing-room, on the sofa. Oh, what about you, Celia? Did you bring a costume? Do you want to change?'

'I've got a bikini on under this,' Celia said, 'But I brought a swimming-costume with me on instructions.'

'Oh my God, Charlie,' Rain said in mock exasperation, 'don't say you're going to initiate another poor innocent into that torture? Did he tell you he was taking you wind-surfing?'

'Yes – why?'

'It's murder. You'll end up black-and-blue from falling about and being knocked by flying floats, and when you're exhausted he'll leap on you in the shallows and you won't be able to resist; you'll feel like a jelly-fish.'

'It's the only way I can get girls into bed with me,' Max grinned evilly. 'I used to club 'em and drag 'em, but nowadays one has to be more subtle. Come on, Celia, you'd better get changed up here. But bring your bikini with you – you might want to sun-bathe afterwards.'

'Lucky girl,' Rain said shortly. 'I daren't sunbathe here – I daren't get white marks or the make-up girls go completely spare.'

'You should stop letting them make you take all your clothes off on films, ducky,' Chris said with complete lack of sympathy.

'What else can I do?' she said. 'I've made a small fortune out of being a sex-symbol. No one's going to cast me as a nun or Joan of Arc.'

'Not until you start sagging, my pet,' Chris said. 'Then they'll begin to notice you can act as well.'

'A good job you added that last bit,' Rain said, and arguing amicably they wandered off down the path.

'I'll go on ahead,' Max said to Celia. 'Come down as soon as you're ready. Just follow the path – it doesn't go anywhere else, you can't get lost. And hurry up, won't you?'

'My, you are eager for my company,' Celia mocked, and for a second he looked at her seriously.

'Yes, I am,' he said, and turned and ran after the others. Celia went inside and changed in the bathroom, wondering what he had meant. She wouldn't mind betting it was a part of the Maxwell Prior routine; unfortunately for him she wasn't susceptible to anything but sincerity.

SIX

The white-gold sand of the beach was scattered with the various bits of paraphernalia without which the wealthy seem to find it difficult to enjoy a day by the sea: deck-chairs, rugs, air-beds, two low tables and one high one, umbrellas, a food hamper, and a refrigerated box large enough to hold a dozen bottles of wine and a meal for six. When Celia arrived the others had already stripped off. Rain was lounging in a deck-chair under the shade of a huge, striped umbrella, resplendent in her fine figure and a tiny turquoise bikini whose purpose seemed to be to expose rather than conceal. Her magnificent hair was held back from her face with a matching silk scarf, and her face was hidden behind a huge pair of sunglasses with white frames.

Chris, his hair looking acid-yellow in the unkindly harsh sunlight, was kneeling beside her deck-chair while she rubbed oil into his back, with dreamy circular movements that seemed to have worked them both into a state of lethargy. He was wearing bathing-trunks so scantily cut that at first Celia thought he must be naked, until she saw across his upper thigh the thin coffee-coloured cord that attached the front triangle to the back. He looked up as she reached the group and smiled at her.

'I see you have no doubts about exposing yourself to the sun,' Celia said pleasantly. 'You obviously aren't worried about white marks.'

'Oh, the directors like the manly torso to be baked a nice light brown,' Chris replied, easing his rippling back muscles into a more ecstatic position under Rain's long fingers. 'Besides, dear, one never strips right off. The bits I hide from you I hide from the world. Unfair as it may seem, ducky, full male nudity isn't on with the great GP.'

'You don't exactly hide your naughty bits from everyone,' Rain said more tartly than her languid movements would have suggested possible. 'I should say a good ten per cent of the world's population must have had a squint at them by now.'

'Ooh, bitch bitch bitch,' Chris squeaked. 'You *have* been eating lemons, darling.'

Celia smiled faintly and passed on, dropping her bag and bits and pieces near them and taking only her bathing-cap down to the water's edge. There Max was readying the floats, stripped down to a pair of decent black trunks. He was one of those people, Celia thought, who looked better without their clothes than with. His powerful neck, shoulders and arms balanced better with the rest of his body when you could see it all. He had quite a decent pair of legs, too, had the right amount of hair in the right places, and a pleasant, early-summer tan. He looked trim and fit and athletic and altogether, Celia thought with half a gulp, very fanciable.

He looked up at her approach and smiled welcomingly, as if she was the one person in the world he wanted to see. Careful, Celia told herself, don't let him charm you. Remember he only wanted you here today because – a puzzling stop. She still didn't know why.

'There you are!' he cried. 'Now, I'm going to initiate you into one of the best experiences of your young life. Let me have a look at you – yes. I approve. You're a very unusual young woman, you know.'

'Why?' Celia asked, joining him thigh-deep in the water and catching hold of the bucking edge of the float. The waves were big and deep and long here: if she hadn't been booked for this wind-surfing business she would have ducked straight under and gone for a long swim.

'Well, you came here today without a scrap of make-up on,' Max said, squinting at her against the sun, 'you've put on a very plain and sensible costume instead of a bikini, and you're even prepared to cover up your beautiful hair with a cap. It's almost as if you don't care about attracting me.'

Celia said shortly, 'I don't, if it's the kind of attraction that depends entirely on my looking like a fashion-plate. If you have to see most of my body and all of my hair before you can like me, I don't think I'll bother.'

Max only smiled. 'When I said you were unusual, I meant it as a compliment. You don't know how tired one can get of being pursued with all the feminine wiles and nothing else. Women seem to think that because one is a film star, they've got to look like Rain Bacchus and it doesn't matter what, if anything, they have in their heads or their hearts.'

'Hearts, Mr Prior? Are you concerned with hearts?' Celia said.

'Please don't be hostile, Celia,' he said, quite gently, and she felt an unexpected and unreasonable pang at the way he said her name. 'I know I more or less blackmailed you into coming here today, but I did want and expect you to enjoy yourself. I hoped you'd be nice to me.'

Now's your chance, Celia said to herself. 'Yes,' she said, 'please tell me just why you asked me here today. I'd like to know.' He looked away from her in a manner that might be termed embarrassed or shifty. 'Well?' she prompted him. He looked briefly at her, and then down, his absurdly long eyelashes shading his eyes from her.

'It sounds so silly,' he said, 'but when I first met you at that stupid party I wanted to get to know you. You fascinated me because you were so different. But of course I didn't know who you were or where to contact you. It seemed like a miracle when you came into that pub, and when you started to walk out and disappear again, I had to do something to get to know you.' He paused a fraction of a second and then looked up, blue-grey eyes under dark lashes gazed piercingly into hers, the sudden flash of blue disarming, taking her aback. 'You see? I did what I did for good reasons, even if I went about it the wrong way.'

Celia suddenly had an image of herself as she would appear to an outsider at that moment, say on a film – standing in the shallows of this beautiful beach under a speedwell-blue sky, beside Maxwell Prior, the film star, the idol of thousands; him looking into her eyes and saying he had wanted to get to know her; two other film stars lounging behind them on the beach. It was absurdly like a scene from a film, and it prevented most of Max's dart getting to her heart – most, but not all. She felt that the most reasonable ending to that scene would be a step forward, a hesitation, and then a lingering kiss, and while most of her laughed at the idea and wondered if actors could ever stop acting, a small part of her would have welcomed the dénouement, if it had happened.

It didn't happen, however. Perhaps Max's timing was too good for that. He said, 'Okay? Well, come on then, let's push this out a bit further, and I'll tell you what to do.'

He gave her a demonstration first, how to sit astride the float until the balance and the wind were right, how to get to her feet without tipping over, how to balance with the sail, leaning in counterbalance to the wind, steering by tipping the wind out of one side or the other. Then he came back to her, panting and wet from the spray, and said,

'Now you have a try. I'll help you. Remember the nearer to straight you can get, the faster you'll go. These things are shaped so there's a very slight keel effect, and if that's biting the water, you'll skate along faster.'

It was a new experience for Celia, slightly scary, very exhilarating. Her sense of balance was excellent, and she was fit and well-muscled, so she had little difficulty in mastering the basic skill. After that they both skimmed about the shallow crescent bay, racing each other, shouting in exhilaration to each other, and sometimes merely enjoying in silence the humming wind that thrust them so fast and effortlessly across the gleaming surface of the water.

They both went in on numerous occasions, coming up spluttering and laughing and clinging to the floats that seemed to take on a perverse life of their own when you came off them. Once they collided on opposite tacks, and came up clinging to each other, both having grabbed for the same float.

'Mermaid!' Max cried. 'I've caught a mermaid! Oh, no it's you. You swim like an eel. Do you do everything as well?'

'Depends what you mean by everything,' Celia panted, trying to keep the lapping green waves out of her mouth.

'I'd love to see you swimming with your beautiful hair floating behind you. It would look like dark golden seaweed,' he said. Celia suddenly became aware of his hands on her upper arms, and even as she did, he slipped his arms further round her and drew her to him. It may look romantic, but it is uncomfortable to be held like that when you're out of your depth. Her legs had been beating a regular rhythm to keep her afloat, and now they were hampered by the nearness of him. She struggled against him.

'It's all right, relax,' he said. 'I've got you.'

'I don't want to be got,' she protested. 'I was all right. I can float on my own.'

He only laughed. 'How childish that sounded. You even look like a child in that bathing cap. But no child ever had a mouth like that.' He kissed her, but it was only a brief touch of the lips, almost a brotherly salute. Then he let her go, and she trod water gratefully, glad to be under her own steam again. Not to be churlish with him, she explained,

'It's like being a driver yourself and having to have someone drive you. When you're a good swimmer, you're never happy being supported in the water.'

'Yes, I know what you mean,' he said, and it was the first normally friendly remark without any overtones or undertones that she could remember him making. He could *be* a good friend, she thought, if ever he could stop acting out his scripts with everyone.

After another couple of turns, they were both panting and in need of a rest, and without reference to each other they turned at the same moment for the shore and, reaching it, beached their floats and flopped down on the hard, shining sand just above the tide-point.

'Well, what did you think of it?' Max asked her, leaning on one elbow to look at her. His eyelashes were stuck together, like a child's who's been crying, and his black hair was slicked down with water and dripping on to the end of his nose.

'Marvellous,' Celia said. 'Great fun.'

'You took to it like a duck to water,' he said. 'You do a lot of sport, don't you?'

'As much as I can,' she said. 'I like to keep fit.'

'I guess you'd pick up things very quickly, judging by how quickly you got the hang of this. Have you ever tried hang-gliding?'

She shook her head. 'I'd love to, though. One day.'

They lay back to rest on the sand, and were roused a short while later by Chris padding towards them with long, cool drinks.

'These are long toms,' he said, handing them the dew-frosted tumblers of pale pink liquid, clinking with ice-cubes and decorated with slices of orange. Celia sipped gratefully, and found it delicious.

'What's in it?' she asked.

'Secret,' Chris beamed delightedly. 'Basis of sloe gin, but other things that only God and I know. And there's fruit and cheese in the box, if you're hungry after your exertions.'

'I am,' Celia said. 'I'll come up.' She got to her feet and padded over the sand with Chris to where Rain was sitting, so Max had no choice but to follow. Shortly Celia was lying on a big rug next to Chris, with a hunk of ripe camembert and a huge yellow peach, out of which she took alternate bites.

'You looked most impressive from here, didn't she Rain?' Chris said. 'You picked it up very quickly. And the cozzy and cap made you look very sportsman-like, like someone entering the Olympics.'

Celia laughed. She had taken off her cap, and her hair was hanging loose behind her as she tilted her head back to look at the sky. 'I'll change into my bikini as soon as I've got the energy. I think that costume has had its fair share of attention. What a glorious blue sky. I can hardly believe I'm here. I'm very grateful to you for bringing me.' She said this to the sky to avoid having to itemize her gratitude.

'I shouldn't be if I were you, dear,' Rain said. 'Gratitude can bugger up your life, can't it, Charlie?'

'You should know, dear,' Max said with automatic venom. He was stretched flat on another rug, eyes closed, drying himself or sunbathing or both.

'Why do you call him Charlie?' Celia summoned the energy to ask.

'That's his name, isn't it, Charlie?' Rain said. Max sat up, looking angry.

'It isn't,' he said. 'I've told you a million times, I changed my name by deed poll. My name is Maxwell Prior.'

'Well, Charlie was your original name wasn't it, Charlie?' Rain continued, unmoved by his anger. She paused, and then said maliciously, 'Charlie's *real* name is Charlie Mandelbaum. Nice name, isn't it?'

'Damn you, Rain,' Max said petulantly, and threw a handful of sand at her. She ducked, laughing.

'Don't do that, Charlie, you'll get it in the food. What's the matter, anyway? Don't you want your nice new friend to know your real name is Charlie Mandelbaum?' The sound of the name suddenly seemed to get to her, and she began to laugh, kicking her legs in the air with delight, feigned or otherwise. 'Charlie Mandelbaum!' she crowed. 'It's too delicious for words!'

'Oh shut up!' Max shouted at her. 'I've told you and told you and told you – ' Suddenly he jumped to his feet. Rain, for all her appearance of being helpless with laughter, was out of her deck-chair in a flash, and running away along the beach towards the edge of the cove where a spit of tumbled rocks divided it from the next, and Max went after her, gradually gaining on her so that, as if it had been planned, he caught up with her just as she scrambled over the rocks and out of sight.

Chris and Celia had watched in silence, and when the other couple had disappeared, Chris rolled over on to his back and sighed, looking contentedly up at the sky.

'Well, that's that,' he said. 'Mission completed. We have served our purpose and, like the first stage of a missile, can drop back into the sea for recovery later.'

Celia looked at him, slightly surprised. 'Sorry?' she said.

'That's all right.' Chris smiled at her from behind his Greek God profile. 'I don't mind. What about you? How does it feel to have accomplished something as wonderful and enduring as bringing those two back together.'

'I don't know,' Celia said patiently. 'You tell me.'

'Didn't you know?' Chris asked innocently. 'Well I certainly knew what I was here for, but I don't mind that. Rain and I – well, we're more like old friends, really. And I'd never say no to a chance of a day at Rain's husband's villa, private plane, lashings of champers, lovely grub, and a bask on the beach. So when she asked me along, I said yes. Who wouldn't? Not you, apparently.'

'Max asked me, for reasons best known to himself,' Celia said shortly. She was beginning to understand what he was implying, but she was not too keen to have it all spelled out. Chris obviously wanted to spell it out, however.

'Max was just a *teeny* bit naughty to do a nasty on a nice young thing like you,' he said. 'He and Rain have had this frightful quarrel, and Rain told him to piss off, in terms no less frank than that, though maybe more expansive. So he came along today with the best-looking bird he could drag up, to make Rain jealous. And it worked. Just as Rain bringing me made Maxie jealous. Now they can get back together, and everyone will be happy.'

So that was it, Celia thought, enlightened at last. It made sense – much more sense than the notion that Max had wanted to make friends with her, damn the expense! She smiled faintly, and Chris, who was watching her out of the corner of his eye, rolled over on to one elbow and looked at her with slight surprise.

'I must say you're taking it very well. Can it be that you don't fancy Maxie after all? That you aren't heart-broken?'

'Disappointed, are you?' Celia suggested.

'Not at all. Now you and I can have some fun together.' And with that he rolled over on top of her and clamped his mouth down on hers in a wet, sloppy kiss. Celia struggled. She was a big, strong girl, but Chris was bigger and heavier and a dancer into the bargain, with a dancer's muscles. She couldn't have shifted him, except that he allowed her to. He rolled off her again, smiling, and she sat up, rubbing her mouth angrily with the back of her hand.

'Don't *do* that,' she spat.

'All right, dear, just testing,' Chris said unconcernedly. 'I couldn't fancy you anyway – you're too butch. I like round, feminine women. No hard feelings, ducks. We'll be spending a bit of time together, so we might as well be friends. Tell me, love, if you don't fancy Maxie, what on earth did you come here with him for?'

'It was a bargain between us,' Celia said. She could think of no reason why it had to be kept secret.

'A bargain? What was that about? Do tell.' Chris sat up, hugging his knees in excitement or perhaps feigned excitement.

'My firm wanted Max to take the lead in a film we're making. He didn't want it, but agreed to take it if I'd spend the day with him here. I couldn't understand why he wanted to spend the day with me, but you've supplied the reason for me. I understand now.'

'My God, I wish people would want me for a film as badly as that. But Maxie's fooled you twice over, darling,' Chris said. 'He needs money badly, that I *do* know, so he'd have taken the part anyway, even if it was second lead to James Bond. He must have been spoofing to hold you off for more cash.'

Celia shrugged. 'Well, whatever the cause, we've got him, and that's all we care about.'

'But tell me, darling, woman of mystery that you are, who *are* you? Who do you work for that wants Maxie enough to throw you in as part of the bargain?'

'I work for Bantham Films,' Celia said. 'I'm producer's assistant. Walter Bruno wanted Max for the part, so I agreed to try and persuade him to take it. It wasn't anything more than that.'

But Chris had stopped listening. He was looking at her with a peculiar expression, grave and thoughtful. 'So that's who you are,' he said slowly. 'Bantham Films.' He looked away down the beach to where Rain and Max had disappeared. 'Bantham Films, he said again. 'Now I understand. So you work for the lovely Simon Davis, do you? You must give him my love next time you see him. We worked together very closely on *Death of a Patriot*, you know.'

'I imagine you did,' Celia said non-committally. 'It was a good film. I thought you were very good in the part.'

'Did you?' Chris said, with unexpected eagerness. 'Did you really?'

'Yes, I did,' Celia said, surprised that his ego should need *her* commendation.

'Perhaps you'd – ' Chris began, and then stopped abruptly.

'Perhaps I'd what?'

'Oh, nothing. No, nothing,' Chris said, relapsing into thought. Then he jumped up with a sudden, false energy. 'Come on, Celia dear, let's try those ballet positions I was doing with Rain on the plane. I'm sure you'd be ever so good at them. Come on, where the sand is nice and firm, down by the water. I want to see if I'm right about you. I pride myself on being able to spot a supple body when I see one.'

They were still practising attitudes when Rain and Max came back along the beach, hand in hand, in perfect friendliness, and, without a word being said by anyone about their disappearance, all four went in for a swim, and played and splashed in the shallows as if they were four children with no more complicated feelings about each other than school-friends might have had. Soon it was time to go up to the house and shower and change, and tea was served on the terrace as before. Then, with what Celia was coming to recognize as characteristic abruptness, Rain said they must be getting back to England.

'Get your belongings, come along, hurry up everyone. Miguel is waiting.'

'I thought we were going to have dinner, Rain,' Chris protested.

'We will, darling, we will, but we'll dine in London. Come along, that's right. We can't dine here, Celia hasn't got a dress with her.' The last was an afterthought, and everyone must have realized it. Chris said no more, and very shortly they were all in the plane and strapping themselves in for the take-off. Celia decided that this energy of Rain's was not energy at all but a chronic restlessness; she had to be continually on the move or boredom got her. It was like being stalked through a jungle from which one couldn't escape by a predator that never tired. Celia pitied her from her heart.

Once back in dear old chilly England, Max drove Celia home and told her firmly that he would wait while she changed.

'I'd rather not join you for dinner,' she said. 'I think I've had enough for one day.'

'I'm sorry, but the bargain is not yet fulfilled. You have to dine with me, stay with me until midnight, or the deal's off. You said you'd spend today with me, and today isn't over yet.' Celia remembered what Chris had said, that Max needed the money and would have taken the part anyway. She wondered if it was true, and why Max wanted her to dine as well. Surely he and Rain had settled their differences along the beach? They had sat together in the plane and talked in whispers to each other like lovers. But it was true that she had agreed to spend the day with him, and if he interpreted the day as up until midnight, she must stand by it.

'All right,' she said. 'I gave my word, and I won't break it. I'll stay with you until midnight.'

'Good girl. Now go and change. Be quick. Put on something really pretty.'

So he still wants to make her jealous, does he? Celia thought as she ran upstairs. Oh well, there was no harm in complying. She washed quickly, brushed her hair, did a lightning make-up job, and then wriggled into a skin-tight turquoise silk Lanvin dress which left a great deal of her to be desired, including most of her back down to her waist. Her choice was approved. As she came downstairs Max gave a soundless whistle.

'You look – fabulous,' he said. 'I mean literally. Like a creature from a fable. I feel proud to be escorting you tonight. Can I use your room to change? I've got my clothes with me. You can fix

73

us both a drink while I demonstrate the art of the quick change.'

He was very quick, and came back down to the ready drinks in dinner-jacket and black tie, looking darkly handsome and distinguished, more like a diplomat than a film star, except for the blue, blue eyes and long dark lashes. We make a handsome couple, Celia thought, and then remembered that they weren't a couple, that her function was to make Max and Rain a couple, for as long as it pleased them to stay together. The idea depressed her a little, and it took all her resolution to be gay and chatty, as if she didn't care about him or the slight to her.

Dinner was a success. They went to the Café Royal, which was a first time for Celia. Chris was in dinner-jacket too, and Rain wore a flame-red chiffon dress of the only shade which would not clash with her hair. It was brilliantly chosen, and Celia admired the flair that could choose a red dress to go with red hair, rather than the usual safe blues. People gathered to stare as they went into the Café Royal, and there were murmurs of recognition, and from somewhere the flash of a camera – some reporter had happened to be in the right spot at the right time; or perhaps it was a gossip columnist, doing his usual round. Celia savoured the amusement of entering the Café Royal with *three* film stars at once.

The food was marvellous, and Celia was hungry enough after her strenuous day to enjoy it thoroughly. The talk was lively and sparkling, and, as it had been on the beach just before they left Spain, there was no pairing off, all four of them talking and laughing together like old friends. For the time being, Celia could forget she was the outsider; even Rain was friendly to her, once or twice leaning over to her and touching her as she spoke, as Celia had seen her do to both men. She was sorry when the evening was over, and her short sally into the realms of high society had ended. They left the restaurant at eleven-forty, and Max said to Celia as they waited in the foyer for their car to be brought up,

'I may have a job getting your back to your house by midnight. You won't turn into a frog if we're a few minutes over the stroke of twelve, will you?'

Celia smiled up at him. 'No. I don't mind. I'm enjoying myself.'

'Are you?' he said eagerly, smiling down at her. His hand found

74

hers and squeezed it, and for a moment Celia forgot his duplicity. Then the car came and the commissionaire was helping her in with a respectful touch of his topper, as if she were a film star too. Well, for all he knew, she might have been. One couldn't recognize everybody, after all.

The drive back to Chiswick was done in silence. Max's first remark was as they drove along the Mall. 'Tide's out,' he remarked. 'How lucky you are to live here. I've always admired these houses.'

'Yes, I am lucky,' she said contentedly.

He glanced at her. 'You've had a nice day?'

'On the whole, yes,' she said, adding, in case he should ask what whole, 'I enjoyed the wind-surfing.'

'I thought you would. We must do some more things together. You must go riding with me, sometime soon. I don't want you slipping out of my life now I've found you.'

They had stopped outside Celia's house now, and she turned to him with surprise at these words.

'Don't be silly,' she said. 'You'll probably be seeing more of me than you want, once we start reading-through and filming.'

'Oh yes. I'd forgotten,' Max said, with a wry twist of the mouth. He got out of the car, came round to let her out and walked with her to the door of her house.

'I won't ask you in,' she said, 'as it's so late, and I have to be up early for work tomorrow. Thank you for a pleasant day. We'll be in touch with your agent to agree terms.'

He looked almost comically dismayed. 'Celia, why so cold all of a sudden? It wasn't all for business, was it? Is that really why you came with me?'

She looked almost contemptuously at him. 'I shouldn't waste my best lines if I were you. Save them for Rain. You only wanted me along to make her jealous, so you needn't pretend it was anything to do with me personally.'

'Is that what you think?'

'Chris explained to me.'

'Chris. Ah yes. It didn't occur to you, then, that *he* was jealous of me and wanted to get you away from me?'

Celia's mind reeled. It was all getting too involved. She said firmly, 'Let's just stick to the facts, shall we? I agreed to spend a day with you so that you would take the part in the film. We are from different worlds, you and I, that have nothing to do with each other. You don't care for me and I don't care for you.'

'Don't you?' he asked. She was furious at his conceit.

'Other people's left-overs? No thank you. I can do better for myself than that.'

Now he was angry. She saw *that* barb go home, and his nostrils flared with anger. Without a word he seized her in a powerful grip, and his mouth came down on hers, his tongue pressing against her teeth, forcing entry. She felt the heat of his body pressing against hers though the thin material of her dress. An unreasonable, irresistible pang struck her in the pit of her stomach, and suddenly she yielded, her tongue came up to meet his, and she slid her arms round his neck to pull him to her. He made a small sound like a groan, and his tongue thrust deep into her mouth, while his hard, hot body pressed against her.

Desire made her dizzy; she wanted him fiercely, more than anyone ever before. His hand released itself from her back and dipped down into the low neck of her dress, surrounding and lifting one breast, pinching the ready nipple between his finger and thumb. Celia heard herself moan, but the sound was far away behind the drumming beat of her blood and his. She had to have him; they had to have each other. She knew that in a moment or two he would stop kissing her and she would take his hand and lead him into her house and upstairs. Foreknowledge of desire fulfilled increased her avidity. She pressed against him, feeling the instant reaction as his penis hardened.

And then suddenly it stopped. He pushed and pulled himself back from her, holding her by the upper arms to steady her, or himself, or both. It was like something being pulled out by the roots to have it stop there. Her maddened body yelled for the sensations not to stop. She stared at him, panting, her eyes half-glazed with desire. His face was red, suffused with blood, and he too seemed dazed, but he said roughly, 'No, Celia. No more.'

'What?' she muttered, coming to gradually. She shook her head, as if to clear it. He was coming back to normal, and a small, rather hard smile crossed his face.

'No. I won't do it. I told you yesterday that I had no designs on your body. That was a lie. But I also promised I wouldn't touch you, and I value my word as you apparently do. Never let it be said that Charlie Mandelbaum went back on his word. You shall go back safe into your house in the same condition you left it.' He turned her round and gave her a little push towards her door.

She looked at him over her shoulder, and he turned away with a little wave of the hand that looked somehow forlorn.

'Good night, Celia. God bless you. Thank you for giving me a day of your life,' he said, and without another glance he got into his car and drove away.

SEVEN

Struggling up from the depths of a puzzling and difficult dream to find the telephone ringing, Celia knew instantly that it was Max. She reached out for the receiver of the bedside extension, and her eye sought the clock to find it was nine already – she had slept the sleep of the idle rich, drugged with food and wine; the dream was the result of frustrated desire.

'What do you want?' she said abruptly into the mouth-piece.

'Celia?'

'Yes. Sorry, Simon, I didn't think it was you.' She struggled into a sitting position, rubbing her free hand over her face to awaken herself.

'Did I wake you up? I'm sorry to phone so early, but I wanted to find out if you were all right.'

'It isn't so early – in fact, I'm going to be late for work.'

'Don't worry about that. Are you all right, that's the main thing?'

'Of course I am. Why shouldn't I be?'

'I've been cursing myself for letting you do it. It was quite unnecessary, and tasteless of Walter to suggest it, but worse of me to let you do it.'

'It's all right, Simon. After all, I could have refused.'

'You shouldn't have been put in that position,' Simon said, and she could hear the genuine concern in his voice. It was nice of him to take this fatherly interest in her, but she had been independent so long that it had to seem rather silly and superfluous to her. 'And I'm ashamed, feeling as I do about you, that I – '

'It's all right,' she said again through a yawn that partially deafened her. 'We had a day on the beach and went to the Café Royal for dinner, and he behaved quite correctly. He was as good as his word – he only wanted my company.' Hearing from the quality of the silence that Simon was not convinced, she added, 'I understand from a reliable source that he wanted me to make his ex-girlfriend jealous, that's all.'

'Well, if that's the case – if you're sure – '

'Where shall I come to work this morning?' Celia asked firmly, to end the matter. 'To the office?'

'Go back to sleep, if you had a late night. No hurry for anything. And when you feel ready, ring me up at home. I'd like to go through the script with you on one or two things. I'll be speaking to Walter this morning, and he'll probably bring some points up too. If it's a nice day we might go out somewhere in the car and do our work beside the river, or something.'

'That'll be nice, Simon,' she said vaguely. 'I think I'll take you up on that extra sleep, though. I feel battered. Jet-lag, I suppose.'

'All right. Ring me when you wake up, Celia darling.'

She barely heard him, and murmuring good night in her sleepiness, she put the receiver down and huddled back under the bedclothes. When the phone rang again it dragged her up from a far greater depth, and she felt far worse. It took her a long time to come to enough to sit up and reach for the phone, cursing it, and seeing that this time it was a quarter to ten.

'Hello,' she said crossly.

'Good morning, my darling. I was just going to hang up and try you at the office. Your master has let you stay home today to recover, has he?'

The first words had caused an unregulated bounding of the pulse at the sound of Max's voice, but it was quickly followed by the irritation of being woken again so soon.

'I was asleep. You woke me up,' Celia said.

'Never mind. You have all your life to sleep in. Today is a beautiful day, as you will see if you take off your lavender silk sleeping-mask and press the button which opens your curtains by remote control – '

'I'm in no mood for all this,' Celia interrupted him ungraciously. 'What do you want?'

He became abruptly business-like. 'I want to arrange our little outing.'

'What little outing?'

'We're going riding together, don't you remember?'

'I never agreed to anything of the sort,' Celia said sharply. 'Our bargain was for yesterday only. I don't know why you're playing games with me – '

'Dear Celia, how ungracious you are. You must be one of those people who wake in a bad humour. All right, our bargain expired on the stroke of midnight, but that's no reason why we can't renew it, is it?'

79

'I'm not a library book,' Celia said. 'I'm supposed to have some say in who takes me out.'

'Of course you do, darling, whoever denied it? We had a lovely day yesterday and enjoyed each other's company and we want to see each other again.'

'I don't want to see you again.'

'Yes you do, darling, don't tell lies. You didn't slap my face at all convincingly last night. Why are you being so unreasonable?'

As soon as he said it, she felt she *was* being. That was the power of his acting technique, she told herself. All the same, she *had* enjoyed herself – she must explain politely, she owed him that much.

'Look, Max,' she said, and he interrupted with a deep groan.

'Celia, *do* be careful! I've heard more sentences beginning "Look Max" than you've had champagne breakfasts, and they've all turned out to contain something absolutely unforgiveable.' Celia tried to ignore this.

'As I said, I don't know why you are pretending to be taken with me, but it doesn't fool me. I don't know why you wanted to spend the day with me yesterday if it wasn't for the reason Chris suggested, but you must see that you and I are from different worlds, which can have nothing to do with each other – '

'Celia, Celia, you can't say things like that, you really can't. Before the war, or in bad fiction, yes, but not in real life. You've been reading too many magazines, darling. Different worlds, indeed. I might expect you to be uninformed, but narrow-minded and priggish I certainly did not think to find you.'

Celia kept her temper. 'All I can say, then, is that you'll soon be seeing more of me than you perhaps want, once we start the pre-filming. I don't think it's a good idea to mix business and social life. I've done it before and it was a very bad idea indeed. And now, if you don't mind, I must get up and get ready for work.' She removed the receiver from her ear and replaced it only for long enough to say, as politely as possible, 'Goodbye,' and then rang off.

She was sitting by the french windows eating toast and jam and reading the newspaper when the phone rang again. This time she took it on the sitting-room extension with a mixture of resignation and apprehension; but it turned out to be Simon again.

'Celia, I hope I didn't wake you again?'

'No, I'm up, having breakfast. What's the matter?'

'Panic stations, I'm afraid. Can you come in to the office? Bill's already there.'

'Of course. I can be there in – three quarters of an hour, say.'

'Good girl. Don't break your neck, but – '

'What's the problem, anyway?'

'Walter – changing his mind. Or at least his schedule. It isn't his fault, but he won't be able to be around for the winter shooting of the hunting scenes, so we'll have to fit it in now.'

'But, Simon – '

'I'll explain all when you get to the office. I have to do some phoning now, so I must ring off.'

'All right,' Celia said. 'I'll see you later.' She put the phone down, and wondered once more at the stupidity of directors, who could not grasp the simplest fact of life, such as the fact that it was impossible to shoot winter hunting scenes in warm spring weather. She finished her toast quickly, and went to shower and dress.

Bill greeted her with expansive pleasure when she arrived at the office.

'What a joy to see a smiling face,' he said. 'Jean's in a foul mood today.'

'Why, what have you done to her?' Celia asked. Jean was Bill's wife, a most long-suffering woman from what Celia could gather.

'Oh, you assume straight away it was my fault,' Bill said, pretending to be offended. 'All I did was ask her to iron me a shirt, and she went right off at the deep end.'

'I should think so too,' Celia said. 'Why should she iron your shirts for you? She goes out to work all day, the same as you.'

'But she's better at ironing than I am. It seems only reasonable that we should do what we're best at. I'm better than her at changing fuses – '

'I hope you didn't try that old chestnut on her,' Celia grinned. 'You don't have seven fuses a week to change, now do you?'

'That's exactly what Jean said,' Bill said gloomily. 'Just like a woman – you always stick together.'

'Garn,' Celia said, ruffling his hair as she passed. 'You can't bait me. Is Simon here yet?'

'Yes, he's here,' Simon called from his room, and Celia went in.

'Now, Simon,' she said firmly. He lifted his hands.

'I know, I know. Sit down, let me tell you.' She sat, with an air of one who is not going to be convinced against her will. 'Walter can't wait until next winter to film the hunting scenes. He took and accepted your point about the season. But he has discovered that point-to-pointing goes on until early summer, so he says why not change the hunting to point-to-pointing and film it now, before we go to Greece.'

'Did they point-to-point in those days?' Celia asked.

'Apparently they did. And the scene transfers without much difficulty. You have to cut only the hunting dialogue, and that isn't essential anyway. The important bit, the meeting on horse-back and the fall, work just as well. So what we've got to do is hurry everything through and book everything for the filming by the end of the month.'

'We haven't even got a leading lady yet,' Celia reminded him.

'We have – sorry, that's another thing you didn't know. We found her yesterday. A young lady by the name of Fern Hastings – '

'What?'

'Oh yes, it is her real name. She's perfect as far as looks go, and she has bags of talent she hasn't used yet. She's been doing experimental theatre and TV ads – ripe for "spotting". She did a very good audition for me yesterday morning, and I got straight on to Walter. Fortunately, he was in London, and I took her to see him in the afternoon. He liked her straight away.'

'My God, things move fast with you, don't they?' Celia said.

'Not quite everything,' Simon said mysteriously. He turned his face away from her, and hid it by rummaging in his desk drawer after something, and said, 'But I also did a bit of recruiting this morning – I suppose you could call that quick work.'

'Who have you got?'

'I've got someone for the villain's part, Andreos. Someone you know, actually.' He looked elaborately casual, and Celia stared at him quizzically. 'Chris Shalako.'

Questions seethed in Celia's mind; questions and surmises. Why was Simon embarrassed by this? Why had he given the part to Chris? Had Chris asked for it? Was he blackmailing Simon? What was the relationship between them? Had Chris phoned this morning in consequence of yesterday's outing? But all she asked was, 'What does Walter think about that? It's his prerogative, isn't it?'

Simon looked up at her, and she wondered if she detected a tinge of relief that she hadn't asked anything else. Simon's bright blue eyes looked straight into hers. 'Walter's delighted,' he said. 'He liked Chris in *Patriot* and he's only too pleased that I've got the contact with him.' He shut his desk drawer without having found whatever it was he was looking for, and placed his hands on the desk top with the air of one getting down to business. 'Now, this filming – with a bit of luck we should manage to get it done in four or five days. You and I will have to go over the script and drop all the references to foxes and hounds and so on, and see that the dialogue between Madeleine and Charles is – '

'*Madeleine* and Charles?' Celia interrupted suddenly. 'I hadn't understood – you don't mean you're having *her* riding in a point-to-point?'

'Of course,' Simon said. 'To have that scene between them is essential.'

'But women didn't. They hunted, but I'm sure as a gun they didn't point-to-point.'

'Well, I'm afraid she's going to in this film. Don't worry about it too much, Celia. The audience won't know any better than I did, and the scene will be very effective.'

Celia shrugged. 'Oh well, I can only advise. Where are you going to shoot it?'

'There's a field out near Denham where we usually shoot that kind of scene. Bill's got the number – he'll get on to them and book it. What you'll have to do is ring round the extras and find out how many of them can ride. We'll need ten or a dozen, and they'll need to be reasonable riders, able to jump without falling off. Max Prior, fortunately, is a first-class rider.'

'So I understand,' Celia said drily. Simon cocked his head enquiringly, but she didn't elaborate. 'What about accommodation?'

'No problem,' Simon said. 'Denham is near enough to London for everyone to travel in, and there's plenty of space for the caravans. Anyway, don't you worry too much about that side of things – Bill will do all the routine stuff, but I do want you to handle the extras. You seem to have the measure of them.'

She grinned. 'That's the advantage of being female. Most men still have inhibitions about being bloody to me, however bloody I may be being to them.'

'Hm,' Simon said with a smile. 'I'm not sure if I like the tactic, but I approve of its effectiveness.'

There was so little actual dialogue in the hunting scenes that they did not bother to have a read-through beforehand except for Charles and Madeleine – Max Prior and Fern Hastings – and that was done with Simon alone at his flat, so it was not until she arrived for the first day's filming in the grounds of a large house near Denham that Celia met Max Prior again. He had not phoned her again, and she decided that he had accepted her rebuff at face value and had dropped whatever had been his idea.

The first morning was cold enough to have filmed a hunting scene, had the state of the trees been right, and once she had been round to check with the gaffer that the crews were all present and correct, with the heads of Make-up and Wardrobe that all was well in their caravans, and with the woman in charge of the horses she had hired (from a stable that specialized in horses for film work – another invaluable phone number in Bill's little black book) that they were all alive and well, she was glad to retire to the shelter of their van for a mug of tea and the traditional bacon rolls.

'Everything all right?' Simon asked, looking up from his consultation with Walter Bruno.

'Yes, except that Max Prior hasn't arrived yet, and one of the horses has got a cough. You may have some cutting to do.'

Simon smiled briefly. 'We'll dub the running scenes for sound anyway.'

'You can *see* it coughing,' Celia said. 'It stops dead and hunches its back up like a cat throwing up. Still, it may get better once the air warms up. What about Max Prior?'

'I'll get Bill to phone his flat – oh, no need, that looks like his car now.' Simon leaned out of the caravan window and said, 'Yes, that's him all right. Go and chivvy him, Celia, give him a tongue-lashing. Luckily we can shoot the extras first.'

'I will not,' she said briefly. 'Extras I'll chastise, but not the characters. That's for you. Anyway – ' She left the rest unsaid, and with a nod of agreement Simon went out to speak to Max himself. Celia watched from the window, her bacon roll cooling, forgotten in her hand. That distant figure, stopping to speak to Simon, was doubly familiar, familiar on the one hand as Max Prior the film star, her one-time pin-up, but now also familiar as a man she knew and had spent a long day with, had kissed, and had desired. She wondered what she would feel when she came face to face with him again. At a distance he looked marvellously attractive and desirable, but in her mind was the image of a famous film star who, whatever he said about narrow-minded prejudices, came from a different kind of world from her, and one in which she could have no place.

She had no time for further reflections, for she was interrupted by a crisis in the shape of Fern Hastings, who, already dressed in the beautiful but cumbersome riding habit of an Edwardian lady and holding a hat with a curled feather in it in one hand, appeared at the door of the caravan and said to Celia in her husky, rather breathless-sounding voice,

'I say, I've just discovered that they mean me to ride in the next scene. I can't ride, particularly not side-saddle. I think I could just about stay on if the horse was standing still and someone was holding it, but if it moved an inch I'd fall right off.'

Celia registered horror and incredulity, and then said, 'Wait here. I'll fetch Simon.'

Simon, presented with the news, put his hand to his head. 'It never occurred to me to ask. My God, I must be slipping. I suppose knowing Max could ride, I just never thought about it. *Mea culpa. Mea culpa.*'

Celia gave him a wry smile. 'I'm surprised at you, Simon.'

'I'm surprised at myself,' he admitted. 'But what's to be done? Walter, can we fake it?'

Walter shrugged. 'But of course, we can fake the close-ups. We can put her on the back of a van and film her head-and-shoulders against the trees. But we must have a woman riding in the distance shots. I do not see how we can omit them. She is supposed to ride neck and neck with this *Charles*.' His voice conveyed his contempt for the name, 'and someone we must have, riding side-saddle, and jumping the fences.'

'Couldn't you hang on enough to jump a couple of low hedges?' Simon appealed to Fern. She shook her head, her wide violet eyes opening in horror.

'Oh no, Simon, no way! I'd come right off. And even if I didn't, it would look awful, me hanging on with my arms round the beast's neck.' She shook her head again. 'Besides,' she added frankly, 'I'd be too scared. I don't think you could pay me enough to do it in the first place.'

Max joined them at that moment, dressed and made up but minus his face-hair. 'What's the problem? I smell a conclave,' he said. Simon explained tersely.

'Fern can't ride.'

'No,' Max said. 'But Celia can.' All eyes turned on Celia, and she found herself blushing furiously, not at the sudden attention but at the thought that somehow Max had engineered this. A moment later she told herself that was ridiculous – he could not have known that they would choose a non-rider for the part of Madeleine.

'Can you?' Simon asked. Celia nodded unwillingly.

'Side-saddle?' Walter asked her hopefully.

'I have ridden side-saddle,' Celia said.

'Well enough to jump a few fences?' Simon asked.

'I don't guarantee I might not need a few attempts,' Celia said.

'Well, why didn't you say so immediately?' Simon asked. 'You really are a treasure, Celia. I never realized when I chose you just how marvellous you were.'

'As I remember, I chose you,' Celia said. 'I suppose I'll have to do it. Unless you'll consider rewriting the scene. I did say that I'm sure Edwardian women didn't ride in point-to-points.'

'But no, Celia, this is a much better solution. You shall do this for me, as a favour, and I shall be very grateful,' Walter said.

'No good, Celia,' Max said quietly. 'You're booked. You should have lied when you were asked the first question. I said all along you'd come riding with me, and you see I'm right. You'll discover as you go along that I almost always am. Keep it in mind – you'll find it a very beautiful and inspiring thought.'

Simon, meanwhile, was getting restless. 'You'd better go along and get dressed and made up, Celia. I'm afraid you'll have to give her the costume, Fern, for today, until Wardrobe can get a duplicate made up. Have a word with them about that, Celia, while you're over there. Off you go, and we'll do some of the extra scenes while you're getting ready.'

Celia sighed, and set off across the field to the costume caravan. Max followed her with Fern, and caught up with her at the caravan steps, pausing to speak to her while Fern went on up to get out of the costume she had just got into.

'It's going to take a bit of altering to get you and Fern to share that costume,' he said, and Celia looked at him with what she hoped was an expressionless face, trying not to show how much standing this close to him disturbed her.

'Not all that much,' she retorted. 'We're about the same height and weight.'

'Yes,' Max agreed. 'But Fern hasn't got your attributes. She hasn't anything like these, for instance.'

His body shielded her from view of anyone else as he placed his hands over her breasts in a gesture part carressive, part supportive, like a market gardener testing the quality and weight of two perfect peaches. Celia bit her lip but made no move nor sound. He said gently,

'Now is the moment when, if we were on film, you would slap my face. But perhaps you're beginning to realize that we aren't. It's real life. I want you, Celia, and I mean to have you.'

She met his eyes, and they were not appraising, nor mocking, nor cocky, but only kind and questioning.

'I want you, too,' she said abruptly, 'but I don't know if I want to do anything about it.' And she jerked herself away from him and ran up the caravan steps like someone escaping, but not quickly enough to avoid hearing him say,

'I think you'll have to.'

EIGHT

While Wardrobe was skilfully letting out the seams of the dark-green serge habit, Joan, the make-up artist, did a quick job on Celia's face and hair.

'Since you're only going to be background fuzz, I won't bother too much with the make-up,' she told Celia as her busy hands flew about. 'The nuisance of it is, Fern's using her own hair, and no two blondes are the same colour. Oh well, we must do what we can. If the audience notices, good for them. By the way, did you see your picture in the paper?'

'What picture? What paper?' Celia asked.

'Centre page of the *Comet*. You know, the gossip column – or in their case, four columns.'

'I don't read it,' Celia said.

'Does anyone?' Joan said lightly. 'Someone brought it in and left it – one of the lighting men, I think – and your name happened to catch my eye – you know the way it does. Picture of you going into the Café Royal dolled up to the nines. Leaning on the arm of Our Kid,' (this was the service units' name for Max Prior), 'and accompanied by two equally illustrious personages.'

'Rain Bacchus and Chris Shalako,' Celia said with a small smile.

'S'right. I didn't know you kept such heavy company. What did Simon think about it? I know he isn't keen on over-much fraternization.'

'What a horrible word,' Celia said. 'Actually, it was all done on Simon's order, and not in the least for pleasure, although – '

'Although don't tell Our Kid that!' Joan finished for her. 'His poor ego would come down thump! Well, the gossip columnists obviously didn't know it was all in the line of duty. The blurb ran on the lines that here was a mystery lady putting Rain Bacchus's eye out.'

'I'm sure they didn't use those words,' Celia laughed.

'Keep still, unless you want crows' feet,' Joan told her, rapping the top of her hair with a make-up brush. 'No, it was done in their usual appalling saccharine style. "Lovely starlet Rain

Bacchus who was heavily tipped to be Mrs Max Prior Number Three appeared bravely unconcerned at the presence on his arm of a beautiful and mysterious blonde" – that sort of bullshit.'

'No more, I shall be sick,' Celia said.

'All right. Shake your head, see if anything falls down. It's got to stand up to being ridden in. All right? Okay, run off and get changed. I'll pin your hat on for you just before you mount.'

'Thanks, Joan.' She left the caravan, and put her head back inside the door only to ask, 'Was Rain Bacchus really going to be married to him?'

'Conscience?' Joan laughed. 'I don't know. Ask the Kid. He's the only one who could tell you that. But I think she's already married. Not that that means much nowadays.'

The horse they gave Celia, Duke, was a handsome chestnut gelding, with a blond mane and tail which she discovered on brief acquaintance with him was dyed. His groom held him, stroking his neck, while Joan pinned on her hat and another helper prepared to hoist her into the saddle.

'Ever ridden a film horse before?' the groom asked. Celia indicated she had not. 'He knows his business, but he's used to a firm feel on his mouth – especially since you're riding side-saddle. I don't mean you should hang on to it, but keep a good firm feel all the time, and you'll be okay.'

'What's he like to jump?' Celia asked, a shade nervously. She had ridden side-saddle only three or four times, and jumped, to her memory, only twice.

'Like a flying armchair,' the groom said. 'Aren't you, Duke?' The horse opened one eye at the sound of his name and shut it again.

'Duke?' Celia queried.

'After John Wayne. He's half-brother to Bo that John Wayne rode in *True Grit*.'

'I'm honoured,' Celia said. There was obviously an inner circle even amongst horses. Her hat fixed, she was heaved inelegantly into the saddle, and once she had arranged herself and gathered the reins, Joan came to settle her habit around her. Then Celia tapped Duke with her heel and clicked to him, and he walked off obediently to where Max was, already mounted, on a black with three white socks and a crooked race. Simon and Walter were standing beside him.

'How do you feel, Celia?' Simon asked her anxiously as she

joined the group. 'Comfortable?'

'I think so,' she said, leaning forward to turn a piece of peroxided mane back to the right side with her gloved hand.

'You look fabulous,' Max said. 'I knew we'd go riding together one day, though I didn't think it would be dressed like this.'

'To business,' Walter said, preventing any answer to this remark. 'I think first you go round the course twice, to get used to the horses. Canter the first time round, and gallop the second, and try to keep them close. Then we'll do the race. We'll film it all,' he added to Simon. 'Galloping horses always come in useful some time or other. Right, off you go, then. You know the course?'

They both nodded, and with a glance at each other they turned their horses and moved away to the corner of the field where they were supposed, in the film, to emerge from the wood. There they waited with their eyes on the small group of cameramen for the starting-signal, which was a wave of a handkerchief. On the signal, Max startled Celia considerably by yelling a kind of muted battle-cry as he thumped his heels into the black, and the horse responded by leaping directly into a canter. Celia's horse leapt forward too, almost unseating her, and they were off down the field at an extended canter, Duke a head and neck behind the black, well up into his bridle but not pulling. Celia's nerves disappeared. Duke's action was so smooth that she had no trouble in sitting his canter, even in the unfamiliar side-saddle position, and his steady firmness in his bridle gave her the confidence that she could stop him instantly if she wanted, or turn him, or in fact do anything with him. He certainly was well-trained.

Max, ahead of her, was sitting well down in the saddle, going with the black's movement with the supple ease of a practised horseman. She smiled to herself, thinking that he looked nothing like an Edwardian gentleman, despite the clothes and the face-hair, for no Edwardian gentleman ever rode with that neat 'forward seat'. The chestnut kept up his effortless pace, and they completed the first round and started the second at a gallop, with Celia always slightly behind Max. When they pulled up their horses and rode back to Walter and Simon, the horses were barely panting.

'My God, but they're fit,' Celia said, more breathless herself than the horse was.

'How was it?' Simon asked.

'Piece of cake,' she boasted, smiling. 'As the groom said, it's like riding an armchair.'

'You didn't feel you might fall off? You didn't look insecure,' Simon added quickly.

'No, I felt fine.'

'You looked good,' Max said to her, and she wondered for a moment whether she ought to say he didn't look anything like an Edwardian rider, but decided against it. The whole of this scene, for her money, would be unrealistic. At this stage there seemed no point in trying to correct Max's style.

Joan and the wardrobe girl came running up to re-secure hair and clothes, and while they were thus engaged Walter gave them instructions about the shooting of the actual race sequence.

'You must appear to be urging your horse on, Celia, but you mustn't overtake Max until you are, let us say, five paces from the hedge. You will know how to do that. Max, when you pass the white post, there, you glance back and see her close to you, and you urge your horse on, and for a moment you draw ahead, but she catches you again when you pass the clump of these trees – what are they called, Simon?'

'Silver birches.'

'Good. When you pass the clump of silver birches over there, Celia, you draw level with him again. Then your dialogue. You know the lines, Celia?'

'Yes, of course, but – '

'Say them anyway, in case we can see your lips move. Some of it will be done later in close-up, but I have not yet decided which parts. You must, of course, finish the lines before you reach the overtaking point.'

'Understood.' Max nodded. 'Do you want me to pull back before the jump?'

'No, I think not. Let her overtake you, but as if you still wish to win, yes? Then the jump.'

'Where Madeleine falls off,' Celia said. Walter gave her a small, tight smile.

'Jah, where she falls off. But of course you do not fall off, my dear. You are not a stuntman. The camera will be in the hedge and will shoot from below as you go over the jump, and then we will film again afterwards as Max jumps and finds Madeleine on the ground on the other side. But if you can do it, what I would like is that you drop the reins as you jump and wave your arms as if you are going to fall off. This will make it more convincing when all is put together, yes?'

'Don't take any risks, Celia,' Simon said anxiously. 'If you don't think you can do it, don't.'

'Okay. I'll see how I feel. Are we running through?'

Walter and Simon consulted with a glance. 'It grows late, and the horses are unpredictable elements. I think we shoot straight away. If we have to shoot again, so be it.'

'Okay. You ready, Celia?' Max gathered the reins and turned his horse. 'Remember what you've got to do? And the markers?'

'Yes, I'm all there,' Celia said, and with a nod Max led the way to the wooded corner of the field. This time they stood inside the trees, so that when the signal came they could canter out of the wood into the open as if they were in full flight. Max led the way, thumping his black straight into a gallop and heading up the field at a hell of a lick, so that Celia did not have to pretend to urge her horse on. She had almost forgotten the white post-marker, but her eyes were naturally fixed on Max, ahead of her, and she saw the white flicker of his face as he glanced back, and remembered in time what she was about. With a tiny movement of her hands she checked Duke's stride to allow Max to draw ahead, and then, her eyes on the silver birches, she urged him forward again until they were galloping side by side.

Max glared at her. 'What the hell do you think you're doing?' he shouted angrily. For a second she was startled, thinking she had misunderstood the instructions, and then realized that this was, of course, the first line of their dialogue. Feeling slightly foolish she shouted back,

'You shan't have everything your own way, Charles.'

'You little fool,' he shouted. 'You'll get yourself killed.'

'I'm as good a rider as you are,' she replied. The horses, now they were side by side and not in contention, were slowing slightly, but Celia could still see the hedge she was to jump approaching rapidly. There wasn't going to be time to get the dialogue in. Max's next line should have been, 'But you don't know the way', but instead he yelled at her 'Go on, overtake me. Save the shot.'

Celia picked up his meaning instantly – the dialogue was less important than the action, and could be done in the form of inserted close-ups at the editing stage. She kicked Duke on, and he surged ahead with great strides. Celia gathered him and he took off with professional ease, clearing the broad thorn hedge easily, while Celia remembered in time, as she leaned forward with the jump, to throw her reins away and pretend to grab for Duke's mane. He landed neatly, and she gathered up the reins again and pulled him down to a walk and waited for Max to join her.

'Well done,' he said. 'You reacted like a pro. An actor couldn't have done better.'

'I know you mean that for a compliment,' Celia said, a little breathless from the exertion, 'but not everyone in the world aspires to being an actor.'

'Including most film stars?' he finished for her. 'Is that what you mean?'

'Perish the thought.' She smiled. He grinned back at her engagingly. Really, she thought to herself, he can be terribly charming and attractive at times.

They rode back to Walter. 'Timing no good,' Max called out as they approached. 'Can't get all that dialogue in on that gallop. Do you want to lengthen the gallop or shorten the dialogue?'

'The gallop was good,' Walter said, 'but I'm afraid you'll have to do it again. Cameras two and three weren't happy.' These were the cameras on either side of the hedge. 'I think, cut the dialogue after "You'll get yourself killed." And Celia, you did not catch him up quite soon enough. When he looked back, you were still behind him. I want you to be almost alongside.'

'Yes, okay. It's hard to time it the first time. I'll get it right this time.'

They went back and did it again. This time, Celia put everything she had into it, enjoying herself thoroughly and used enough now to the sequence to be able to react physically at the right moment. They yelled their brief exchange at each other, she drove Duke hard forward, and then fate took a hand. The cameraman was half concealed in the hedge just beside where they were to jump, and the first time Duke had gone over like a bird. Perhaps he hadn't spotted the man hiding the first time; perhaps this time the camera moved, catching the light. Whatever it was, just as Duke took off he was startled, and twisted to one side in mid-jump away from the cameraman. At that same moment Celia had flung away the reins and her balance was slightly impaired. She went one way and Duke went the other, and the next thing she knew the ground was flying upwards to meet her.

Max, seeing her come off, only had time to wrench his horse

hard in the same direction as Duke's swerve, and they took the hedge in a spray of snapping twigs to land just clear of Celia. Max hauled his horse in to a stop that included three bounces, and flung himself off, running clumsily in his riding boots to kneel down beside Celia's prone figure. She was not hurt, just knocked breathless, and was considerably startled to hear Max crying out,

'My darling, my darling!' as he turned her over, lifting her slightly in his arms. His blue eyes bored into hers with some urgent message, and as she was about to speak, she realized, with a lurch of disappointment, that he was 'saving the shot' again. The cameras would have filmed her lucky fall, and the next thing that happened in the scene was that Charles ran back and took her in his arms, saying 'My darling, my darling'. Then he kissed her.

To the cameramen it would probably look like a professional 'stage' kiss. But the warm lips were really on hers, not on her chin, and Max's by now familiar tongue was probing in between her teeth, the taste of him was in her mouth, and one of his hands was hard on her breast, feeling for the nipple through the thick broadcloth. When he lifted his mouth from hers, he murmured as he nuzzled into her hair,

'I'd far sooner be doing this to you than to Fern. I'll bet you fell off on purpose.' Then he kissed her again, thoroughly. Celia wondered what people would be thinking; but they would probably only think that he was concealing her face, which was not Fern's, from the cameras, until he was told that they had stopped filming. All right, she would give him as hard a time as possible. She responded with all her will to his mouth and hands, and felt the quality of surprised pause in what he was doing, before he probed even deeper, his eyes too now closed, his hands gripping her almost painfully.

'Okay, cut,' a voice came from somewhere behind them, and a measurable moment later Max released her and laid her back gently on the grass.

'Sorry about that, but I wanted to save the shot,' he said smoothly. 'Have you got your breath back?'

From the fall or from the kiss? Celia appreciated his double entendre, and replied as evenly as she could, 'Oh yes, it takes more than a little thing like that to knock me.'

As Max stood up, Simon flung himself down on her other side

94

in a passable imitation of someone in a film worried about his beloved taking a toss from a horse. Only, she thought suddenly anxiously, he wasn't an actor.

'Celia, are you all right? I shouldn't have asked you to do it. I don't know what's wrong with me, I keep putting you in these terrible situations. What happened? You shouldn't have tried to fall off, it was too dangerous.'

'Wonderful work, both of you,' Walter said genially, arriving on the spot behind them. 'Wonderful! Celia, you did well to carry on. And Max, you saved the shot, which we couldn't have hoped to repeat. Well done, both of you.'

'I didn't mean to do it,' Celia got out at last, in reply to Simon. 'The horse shied at the cameraman. He must have moved and startled him. You don't think I'd deliberately throw myself off a horse in the path of another, do you? Don't fuss, please, Simon. I'm all right. Just a bit shaken.' And as she said it, she glanced involuntarily towards Max, and saw his answering small smile of complicity.

Celia changed out of the costume and gave it back to Fern, cleaned off the make-up and then went back to the quiet of their own caravan to sit down and drink a mug of hot tea. She would have a couple of bruises, but no horsewoman heeds a fall like that. What shook her more was Max. She knew it was a crazy thing to think, knowing the nature of the beast, but she was sure there was not so much acting in what he did as genuine feeling. Madness! And yet – she remembered his face, his hands, his mouth; she shivered at the memory of the smell of his skin, the taste of him in her mouth. She would have to do something about it all. It was no good.

It began to drizzle lightly, and half an hour afterwards the rain began to come down in earnest, setting in for the day by the look of the sky, and the filming had to be called off. Simon came in, shaking the rain from his hair.

'How are you feeling?'

'Okay,' Celia said. 'It wasn't a bad fall, really. It probably looked worse than it was.'

'Well, filming's off for the rest of the day anyway. I suggest you take the afternoon off, go home and have a hot bath and rest. Shock can do funny things to you.'

'What about the rushes?' Celia said.

'Walter and I will have a look at them this evening. You can see them tomorrow with whatever we get tomorrow, if the rain stops.' He smiled and patted her shoulder. 'You go home and rest. Don't worry about anything.'

He went out again, and Celia waited for the next piece of action in this drama. It came half a minute later. Max came in with a plastic mac thrown over his costume.

'Your place or mine?' he asked simply.

'I'm under orders from the management to go home and have a hot bath,' Celia said.

'Your place, then. I'll change and get this make-up off, and follow you. You go on ahead if you like – I've got my car.'

No question, she noted, from either of them that this time it would happen. She felt her pulse quicken. 'All right,' she said shakily. 'Don't be long.'

'I'll be with you as soon as I can, darling. Fifteen minutes to change, that's all.' He blew her a kiss, and was gone. Still shaking slightly, she got her coat and headed for her car.

After a fast drive home, Celia popped in and out of a hot bath, scented with *Muguet des Bois*, and was in the kitchen, wearing a charcoal-silk wrap with white lace, mulling some wine when the door bell rang. She let Max in without a word, and he followed her to the kitchen equally silently.

'Mulled wine,' she said to him, handing him a mugful. Her voice, she was amazed to hear, sounded entirely natural. He took it, and sipped cautiously, and then took a mouthful. 'Good,' he said. Then he sniffed. 'You've had your bath?'

'Yes.'

'*Muguet*. One of my favourites. I like light, floral perfumes. You, for instance, should wear Balmain's *Vent Vert*.'

'I do, from time to time. But at the moment – '

'Ah, yes, what is that intriguing perfume you wear? I can't place it.'

'It's new. It's called *Vu*.'

'It should perhaps be called *Tu*.' He took another mouthful of wine, then, 'I want to bathe too. I'm sweaty and muddy from the horses, and I can't do you justice unless I feel right. Is there hot water?'

'Yes,' she said. Her voice trembled slightly, and she corrected it. 'You can bathe or shower, as you like. There's a clean towel in the cork-topped box in the bathroom.'

'Right. Finish your wine. I won't be long. Through there?'

'Yes, second on the left.'

She watched him as he walked down the passage, pausing to look in at each door, and turned into the bathroom. She finished her mulled wine, feeling the warm alcohol taking the cricks out of her body, soothing her nerves, and making the edges of the world rosy. The sweet taste of cinnamon was like childhood Christmas distilled, the tang of cloves quasi-medicinal, making all right again. Then he called her from the bathroom.

'Come and wash my back for me.'

He was showering. She had once before seen him naked but for brief swim-trunks. It was amazing how much difference the absence of so small a piece of cloth made. Everything seemed to slow down and race at the same moment; her movements became very deliberate, as if she were drunk.

'You'd better take off your wrap, it will get wet,' he said quietly. She slipped it off her shoulders, and felt his eyes all over her, just as hers were all over him. She stepped in under the warm water and reached out for the soap he held out to her, and passing her arms round behind him began carefully to soap his broad back. Her hands slid over his skin, feeling the wonderful hard silkiness of his muscles. He was incredibly fit, beautifully shaped; without clothes it was impossible to believe he hadn't been the original model for all men. She glanced up into his face, and saw the intensity of his gaze, as if he were concentrating on some very hard problem, the stillness of his face, as if he were waiting for a blessing.

She rubbed lower, feeling the deep cleft of his back where the dorsal muscles stood up in a double ridge, and the hard mounds of his buttocks; then he pulled her arms back from him, and took the soap from her hand, and with delicate, tender movements, as though she were a child, he began to soap her; first her neck, then down and round her breasts, caressingly round the curved underside and up to the nipple, rubbing it and rubbing it until it stood out, hard and ready, reaching out for love.

'Dark pink, like young raspberries,' he said – the first words he had spoken. 'Like little mouths reaching up. See how hard they are.' He flicked them gently with his fingernail, and they grew infinitesimally more rigid. 'They have a life of their own, tiny penises.'

His hands moved on, slipping down the inward curve of her

97

waist. 'You are so beautiful. A little waist I could close my hands round,' he said. And on downwards, gently, thoroughly soaping her thighs. She looked down, and saw how his penis was ready now, thick and hard and taut like a braced muscle, and as his hands touched her at the same moment she felt a warm flood released inside her, making her ready for him. Carefully he gathered her towards him, and slid his hard penis between her thighs, moving it back and forth between the soapy surfaces of her skin in imitation of the act. She began to feel weak with wanting.

'Please – ' she said. He nodded, and, suddenly brisk, rinsed himself off under the water and stepped out of the shower so that she could do the same. He met her with the towel as she stepped out, and patted her dry with care and tenderness, and then, dropping the towel on the floor, he led her from the bathroom into her bedroom next door.

Celia felt weak, and flushed, and shaky, as if she were suffering from a high fever; and in her feeble state, she could only trust Max, wanting him to lead her, command her, make her well. He stripped the covers off the bed in one movement, and gently placed her on the exposed sheet, and lay down beside her.

'Celia,' he said, kissing her cheek and neck. 'Celia. Beautiful Celia, I've waited so long for this, and now I want it to go on for ever. You want me, don't you? *Un peu, beaucoup, passionnement, à la folie, pas du tout?*'

She touched him, hesitatingly, touched the tip of his penis, felt it springing at her touch, not entirely under his control. He moved his mouth downwards from her neck to her breast, drew the nipple into his mouth with his tongue, and she felt unimagined pangs of longing and delight coursing through her as he suckled. She reached for him again, and he put back her hand softly.

'Don't hurry, darling,' he said. 'We have all the time in the world.'

Later he said, 'I wish I could kill the bastard that's been making love to you. Didn't he care about you at all? Don't be so afraid, dearest. I really enjoy doing these things.'

And later again she cried, whimpered, pleading, 'Max, please, now, please, please, come into me.' She was aroused to a pitch that was almost agony, and yet so delightful she could neither bear it to stop nor continue. Max's eyes were narrowed to slits, his breathing was fast and harsh through his nostrils, but only at her request did he ease himself up the bed, and at last, at last, she felt his rock hardness slipping into her. Her breath hissed out between her clenched teeth, her arms folded hard round his back, her feet hooked over his calves, and then they were moving; slow, faster, movements synchronized effortlessly, they were flying, flying, and he swelled to fill her as with a wild cry that might have come from either of them, or both, they reached the top of the incline and were spinning outwards into space and the downy darkness of accomplished delight,

NINE

Outside, the gentle rain continued smokily into the dusk. Max leaned on one elbow, looking down at Celia while his other hand toyed with a length of her hair, running it through his fingers, separating the strands and then smoothing them together again.

'It's like when someone's been driving your car – it just feels different,' he said.

'Or when a bad rider's been riding your horse?' Celia suggested. He smiled briefly.

'Uh-huh. I suppose it's a bit more flattering to liken you to a horse than to a car. Who was he, this bloke?'

Celia shrugged. 'A man I used to work for. He was married.'

'He ought to have known better then,' Max said.

'You can talk,' she said, nettled.

'I didn't mean that, foolish,' he said, amused at her defence of her ex-lover. 'I meant that if he was married, he ought to have had enough practice to treat you like a woman and not like a scratching post. If I knew who he was I'd go and shove his teeth down his throat.'

'Dear me! So savage on my behalf!'

'Why not? You deserve the best there is, not some conceited, half-baked, selfish, heavy-handed – '

'I get the picture,' Celia said, rolling over towards him and kissing him to silence. He caught her to stop her rolling back and, holding her head in his two hands, kissed her deeply and thoroughly.

'There,' he said when he had done. 'That's to remind you he's over and finished with, and only I have the right to do that to you now. Oh Celia! You gave me such a hard time.'

'Did I?' she murmured from her daze of pleasure.

'You know damn well you did. I wanted you from the very beginning, but you were so bound up with this nonsense about actors living in a different world from "real people" that I thought I'd never get through to you. I should have played masterful from the beginning I suppose.'

Celia shook her head. 'No, you shouldn't.' She ran her fingers

100

lovingly over his face, tracing the lines of his jaw and lips. 'This was the right way. Only kindness has the power to move me, I think. I've had enough of the other. You have,' with a quiver in her voice, '*the* most beautiful mouth – '

A long while later they broke apart again, and Max reached out a tender hand to wipe the sweat from her brow. Her expression was dazed, almost bruised with loving. 'You'll wear me out, you know,' he joked gently.

'You aren't that old,' she said, catching his hand and kissing it, with a sigh of contentment.

'Nevertheless, we can't live on love alone. We must have dinner. Where would you like to go?'

'Don't know,' she said, running her hands up and down his sides. He caught them, laughing, and trapped her two hands between his.

'You shall eat, if I have to force it down you. I'll choose. We'll go and shower – separately! – and then I'll choose your clothes, and we'll go and have dinner and just enough wine, and then we'll come back. No arguments – I'm going to be masterful now. Besides, if we make love any more now, you'll be sore, and then we shan't be able to make love all night.'

'And do you plan to?'

'I do,' he said firmly. 'All night, and every night.'

Celia smiled. 'I like the sound of that.'

'That smile is positively indecent,' Max laughed. 'Like a Cow and Gate advert. I'm so glad you like sex, my darling love.'

'Have you known many people who haven't?' Celia asked. He nodded.

'Lots,' he said. 'It's one of the hazards of being famous. Most women cry afterwards, and feel guilty. They say things like, "Now you'll despise me". It makes life very difficult. But why have you got me talking about other women? That's bad manners. Go on, now, and have your shower, while I choose you a dress. Hup! Come on, now.' He urged her up and sent her on the way with a light tap on the buttock, and smiling languorously she went to the bathroom. There was no sense of washing away sin as she stood under the hot water; it was an act of purest pleasure. Her body bloomed under her fingers, seeming different to her already because it had been loved. That, of course, was what *lovely* must mean, she thought.

*

The day before they set off for Athens, Celia received a phone call from Eva.

'Aunty Eva's advice service calling,' she chirruped.

'Don't need any,' Celia trilled back. Eva's voice returned to normal.

'Are you sure you don't, Cely?'

'Of course – why should I?'

'You've been *seen* everywhere with Max Prior, darling.'

'That's because I've *been* everywhere with Max Prior,' Celia replied happily. 'What's wrong with that?'

'Oh, Celia, you don't need me to tell you what's wrong. Or maybe it isn't – maybe you've got yourself a bit of sense from somewhere since I last met you. But really darling, it doesn't look like the act of a sane and healthy mind to involve yourself with a sex super-star, not to mention Rain Bacchus and Chris Shalako, with whom, according to the papers, you've been making a foursome.'

'Evie, I know you are only saying this for my own good, but really, there's no need to worry. I'm having a marvellous time with Max Prior, and he's doing me no harm at all.'

'What do you mean by a marvellous time?' Eva said suspiciously. Celia laughed.

'You don't expect me to tell you all the details, do you? But I will tell you, he has black satin sheets, and gold taps in the bathroom.'

She had been several times to Max's flat, and found it fitted out with the most outrageous 1930's Hollywood-style ostentation, but Max's off-hand amusement with it made it acceptable in him.

'Oh – it's got that far, has it?' Eva said flatly. Celia sighed.

'Darling, what do you think we do with each other? Really! I'm not a groupie, I'm not innocent and seventeen, and I'm not being taken in. I'm in no danger. We are having a nice time together, and everyone approves, even his daily help.' She giggled irrepressibly, thinking of the time she first met the daily help.

She had slept the night with Max at his flat (though slept was both an understatement and an overstatement for what they had been doing all night long; they couldn't keep their hands off each other) and had woken to the startled realization that someone was in the room. Her eyes flew open, and the sight that greeted them was amazing.

He was tall, wafer-thin, with orange punk hair and ear-rings, two to each ear. He was wearing skin-tight pink jeans and a pink satin vest, over which was one of those thin plastic pinafores that nurses wear on maternity wards, and he was bearing a loaded tray from which emanated delightful smells.

'Wakey-wakey!' he trilled. 'Rise and shine, loves. Brekky's here, and it's a lovely day.'

Max woke with a grunt, and roused himself on to his elbow. He seemed not in the least surprised at the intrusion. The stranger pursed his lips and frowned at Max.

'And I must say it was the teeniest bit naughty of you, darling, not to tell me you had a little visitor. No note, nothing! If I hadn't used the old brain-pan and put two and two together I'd be barging in here this morning with only enough brekky for one! Awful!'

Max smiled, and, sitting up properly, performed a proper introduction.

'Celia, may I present Nigel Devenham, my cleaning man. Celia Bancroft.'

Nigel shuddered delicately. 'Sweetie, don't call me that. Makes me sound like a sewer-worker. Daily help is what I like to be called.' He made a bow in Celia's direction. 'Charmed, I'm sure. I hope you like all the same things. With nothing to guide me, I simply made up double of everything that I bring Charlie.'

'Charlie?' Celia murmured, bemused. Nigel straightened up, offended.

'I've been with Mr Mandelbaum for some time,' he said coldly.

'I'm sorry – I didn't mean – ' Celia said, ignorant of her offence. Max reached for the tray.

'Put the tray down, Nigel, and don't be so touchy. Celia didn't mean it.'

Nigel unbent instantly. 'Sorry. But you'd be touchy if you were me.'

'Yes,' Celia mused. 'I probably would.' The tray was set across her and Max's knees. She stared at it with fresh astonishment. Plain yoghurt, muesli, fresh fruit, wholemeal toast, honey, cream, coffee, and two gigantic brown eggs in cockerel egg cups. 'This is marvellous!' she cried spontaneously. Nigel beamed. ·

'Got to keep your strength up, loves!' he said, apparently entirely happy again. 'I'll leave you to it, anyway. Tuck in!' And he willowed out, leaving Celia to wonder if she had hallucinated the whole thing.

'I'm sure everyone doesn't,' Eva said, bringing Celia back to the present. 'What about Simon?'

'Yes,' Celia said thoughtfully. 'I have caught him giving me one or two worried looks during rehearsals, whenever Max comes over to speak to me, or we go off together afterwards. But I think he's only worried in case it affects my work. And I won't let it do that.'

'I don't know that that's why he's worried,' Eva said. 'Haven't you ever wondered if he's not sweet on you.'

'Ghastly expression!' Celia laughed. 'No, I haven't wondered. In fact, your original suggestion has come to mind recently – that he might be gay. Did you know he's wangled a part for Chris Shalako in this film?'

There was a pause while Eva digested this. 'I didn't know that. But I'm sure he's not queer. I've been making enquiries about him, and apparently there was a woman in his past, some kind of bad bust-up, heartbreak and all that, which is why he's not married since. Look, Celia, don't be offended, but do take care, won't you? Don't go falling in love with Max Prior. Remember he's a film star, and they're a breed apart.'

'That's a terrible cliché, Eva,' Celia said.

'There has to be the rule that proves the exception,' she replied darkly, 'and Max Prior is it, if ever there was one.'

'All right, Eva, I'll take care. I won't fall in love with him,' Celia said in the end, to keep Eva happy. But the advice was already too late. How could she help loving someone who loved her so much?

Bantham Films had taken over the whole of the Asterion Hotel, set in a secluded position above a small bay not far from Sounion. Celia had booked it, with helpful advice from Bill, who seemed to know the name and phone number of every hotel in Europe, and had the knack of making himself understood in most languages. Celia had had to carry on her conversations with the hotel staff in a mixture of French and German, these being the two languages besides Greek that they spoke best.

'I'm full of admiration for you,' Simon said one morning coming across her talking polyglot business with the registration clerk. 'I guessed you were talented, but your resourcefulness is wonderful.'

'I shouldn't admire me too much,' Celia smiled back. 'My

French isn't as good as Max's, and my German's execrable. And the camera crews simply shout in English and get served just the same.' It had been meant to make him laugh, but the mention of Max's name brought a frown to Simon's face, and he turned away. He hadn't actually said anything to Celia, but she knew that he didn't like the relationship between her and Max.

It wasn't, she reasoned to herself crossly, that it was interfering with her work. She hadn't come anywhere near guessing how much work there would be for her to do while they were location filming, but she was coping with it with an energy and verve that stemmed partly from her feeling of being loved. She was on the go from dawn until midnight; from the pre-breakfast visits to the sites to check that everything was being set up properly and that things like the light and the tide would be right for what they wanted to do; to the after-dinner sessions with Simon and Walter and one or two of the actors, looking at the day's rushes and deciding with them what, if anything, needed retaking and whether the overall pattern was coming right.

If, after all that, she found time to slip away to the lovely private beach for a swim with Max, and if she spent some part of her night not sleeping but slaking the maddening thirst they had for each other's bodies, what business was that of anyone's?

The first week's filming went excellently, with the minimum of retakes – so excellently that it was decided to knock off after lunch on Sunday so that everyone could have a break and a rest.

'Good job, too,' Chris muttered. 'I'm not a mule.'

'It is the English habit of the weekend that will destroy England,' Walter said solemnly, but everyone knew he was joking. 'However, since you are all tired, I shall use the opportunity to commune with my muse, in preparation for next week. I shall expect you all to work twice as hard when you have rested.'

Simon admitted he could do with a break, not only because he was tired. 'Bill's been nagging me to catch up on some financial business, so I think I'll fly over to Athens this afternoon and get one or two things sorted out,' he said to Celia. 'How about coming with me? You can have a look at the accommodation, and then we could have dinner together. I know a rather nice place – '

Celia, not noticing the wistful note in his voice, said,

'I don't need to look at the accommodation, Simon. It's all

105

arranged, and if you remember, it's the same place that you stayed at three years ago. You don't need me in Athens, do you?'

'You don't want to come?'

'I'm dog tired. I'd sooner spend the afternoon sleeping on the beach,' Celia said.

Simon looked as though he was minded to make some reference to her lack of sleep, but he only shrugged, and said, 'In that case, I think I'll stay over in Athens. You'll all be coming over on Tuesday anyway, and you can cope alone tomorrow, can't you?'

'Certainly, if you want to stay over,' Celia said, pleased at his trust of her. 'I can manage perfectly. Don't worry about a thing.'

'No, I won't,' he said gloomily.

That was how Celia came to find herself spending Sunday afternoon lying on the hot, white sand of the small beach, her head propped against a protruding rock so that she could gaze at the calm, sparkling, lapis-blue sea before her, that touched the curving beach with its lips of white foam and stretched outwards to where the arch of the sky came down to meet it at the silver horizon. Behind her a short, steep cliff of red and grey rocks rose up to meet the hills, thickly wooded with pine, cedar and cypress, interspersed with cultivated groves of olive and citron; the air was aromatic with the fragrance of the exotic herbage and the more familiar perfume of roses and honeysuckle and tender, drooping Wistaria.

Max lay beside her, stretched out on his front to turn his back a shade more golden-brown. His cheek was pillowed on one hand; his other hand lay relaxed across the base of her throat, as if to make sure she did not escape from him while he slept. His dark hair was damp and slightly curling from his latest swim, and there was a crust of salt making a tide-mark across the breadth of his heavy shoulders. Celia watched him through half-closed eyelids, too sleepy and languid to feel more than academically the latent power of him as he lay there, his compact, muscular body relaxed in sleep.

He hadn't been getting much sleep recently, she thought with an inner smile. He had been giving her body a great deal of attention in what time they had spare from the business in hand, and though their pleasure in sex might well be equal, it seemed probable that the exertion involved was not so fairly shared. 'You take a lot out of me,' he had joked one time. And of course he worked hard during the day, often having to act his scenes under the burning sun in most unsuitably heavy Edwardian costumes. 'Every time,' he said, 'I promise myself I'll never do another costume drama. Every time.'

She was glad to discover that he really was a good actor; it touched her pride, now that she was so nearly associated with him. Everyone on the set knew that they were lovers, and it seemed to occasion no surprise from anyone but Simon, and, oddly, Chris Shalako, who annoyed Celia by making continual sly remarks with double meanings. Max shrugged them off and told Celia to ignore Chris. 'He's jealous,' was all he would say. At first the technical crews had watched cautiously to see if Celia would fall down on her work, or if Max would claim privileges on the strength of his relationship with Celia, but when they both continued to work as hard as before, if not harder, everyone relaxed and accepted the situation.

Even Joan, the make-up woman said to Celia, 'I don't know what you've done to Our Kid, but you've certainly improved his temper. I made him up all through *Middlemarch*, and he was rotten fussy. A real little dictator, totally unreasonable when it came to sharing facilities. This week I haven't had a peep out of him.'

It gave Celia a moment's uneasiness, for she remembered that which she had successfully forgotten: Eva's story of how he had gotten Julie Harper taken off the *Sense and Sensibility* production. She decided that there must have been details to that affair that Eva had not been told. She was as sure as she could be of anything that Max was not the kind to act pettishly; as for Joan's experience, it could have been that Max was going through a bad patch. Maybe *Middlemarch* had been filmed while one of his marriages was breaking up, or something like that.

The sun was going down in that absurdly sudden way it does in Greece, as if it was being hauled down hand over hand by some giant sailor out of sight beyond the horizon, and, thinking it was time Max woke, Celia moved slightly to stir him. It worked. His hand tightened slightly on her throat, and then he groaned and shifted and rolled over on to his elbow. He looked at her sleepily, and then smiled.

'Darling,' he said. 'You shouldn't have let me sleep so long.

It's getting dark, and you must be famished. I know I am.'

'I thought you needed the sleep,' Celia said, and he laughed, his new improved tan showing off his white teeth.

'I did, but there's all the time in the world for sleeping. Not enough time for attending properly to you.'

Celia didn't like the sound of that – too finite, as if this were a holiday romance that would end with her return to an office in London and his acceptance of a new bunch of tourists. She shivered suddenly.

'Come on,' he said. 'It's time to shower and dress and have the first cocktail of the evening before seeking out a delicious dinner. As Nigel always says, got to keep your strength up.'

'Oh God yes, Nigel,' Celia said, letting Max pull her to her feet. 'Why did he call you Charlie? Why did you change your name? You know, it occurs to me that I don't know anything about you.'

Now it was Max's turn to shiver. His hand tightened convulsively on hers. 'Don't ask,' he said, and he sounded deadly serious. 'I don't want you to know anything about my past. It's all finished and done with. You are my present. Don't be curious about it, or it will destroy us. Don't ask me anything, anything at all.'

Celia stared at him, a little surprised. She wanted to ask if she was his future as well as his present, but she didn't dare. He took her other hand as well and tried to lighten his words by smiling, but she could see that he was still serious. 'Remember Bluebeard's wife. Don't ask questions, darling, please. Just trust me.'

She nodded, not able to think of anything adequate to say. He put an arm round her and pulled her roughly to him, and began to walk her up the beach. 'That's a good girl,' he said. 'Let's go and have a wonderful hot shower, and put our glad rags on. And, Miss Bancroft, you'll shower alone, in your own room, if you please, otherwise we'll never get to dinner at all.' Celia laughed, and the awkward moment passed.

They ate in the hotel's dining-room overlooking the sea, which turned from blue to molten pewter as the darkness spread over the sky and a sudden moon appeared like part of a backdrop. They ate some delicious grilled fish, with a great plate of Greek salad between them from which they helped themselves; and then came a lamb dish reeking of garlic and tangy with peppers and paprika, and hunks of dark wonderful bread to sop up the gravy.

'Make the most of it,' Max said to Celia, refilling her glass with the resinous local wine. 'You won't get any Greek food in Athens.'

'No?'

'No. Every restaurant serves spaghetti bolognese and American doughnuts and coffee. Gastronomically speaking, Athens is the Catford of the Mediterranean!'

After their meal, they drank tiny cups of bitter Greek coffee, with which was always served a glass of cold water, and sat on the veranda watching the fireflies spin out from the olive groves and dance madly over the surface of the bay. The air was mild and balmy, and scented with night stock.

'Let's swim,' Celia said impulsively. 'Come on – I'm sure we've digested our dinner enough.'

The phosphorescence was bright on the water, so that when they plunged through a wave, it ran like green liquid fire from their bodies, leaving trailers like comets' tails behind them. Under the water, their skin took on a green-gold glow; Max reached out a hand and stroked it along Celia's side with a kind of wonder. Then, quite suddenly, the porpoises were with them, surfacing abruptly from nowhere, filling the bay with their shining humped backs, spilling phosphorescent fire on either side as they cut through the water. They jumped and played all around the swimming couple, seeming close enough to touch and yet never getting quite near enough. Their shining eyes and smiling mouths were everywhere, and the velvet night air was filled with the soft *phoop!* as they cleared their airholes. Celia turned over and over in the water, entranced by them, half-afraid but longing to get nearer to them; and just as suddenly as they had come, they were gone again, leaving the smooth, moon-beaten silver of the water unbroken, as if they had been a dream.

Slowly, they swam to shore, and then rested on their backs in the shallows, looking up at the impossibly near sky.

'The stars look like tiny burn-holes in a piece of black cloth,' Celia said. 'Beautiful – '

'*You* are beautiful,' Max said, and with an upsurge of love at his words Celia rolled over towards him.

'You taste of salt,' Max said a moment later, and began to lick her lips and cheeks and throat. Their wet bodies touched, cold despite the warmth of the night, but heat springing up wherever the two surfaces touched. 'I love you,' Max said simply. They were naked, it seemed, without effort or design, and the wet sand seemed a comfortable bed, and the small waves breaking over them with a sigh and a shrug did not hinder them. They made love there on the tenuous border between the white water and the sea-strand while the sea receded from them. Even as they accomplished their desire, the water had gone back, and when they broke apart at last, they found themselves beached high and dry like flotsam.

TEN

The company was booked into a hotel in Karaiskaki Place, a modern and comfortable building of twin bedrooms *en suite*, each room having a small balcony with a view of Mount Lykavitos straight ahead and, by leaning out and craning the head to the right, a view of the distant and, at night, floodlit Acropolis.

These were the good points. The bad points, from Celia's point of view, were all to do with Athens itself, which she found a great disappointment. She had imagined a fabulously beautiful city of ancient monuments and gracious gardens linked together with tasteful modern additions; what she found was a dirty, shabby, neglected, thoroughly modern city which happened to include a few equally neglected and disintegrating ancient monuments. The streets of the city were quite the worst-paved and dirtiest of any city she had yet been in; the buildings seemed either to be falling down or in process of being put up; and the traffic was the densest and noisiest in the world. All day and all night the vehicles hurtled round Karaiskaki Place, roaring and belching out fumes, with frequent squealings of brakes and fusillades of back-firings, and occasionally an interesting bump-and-grind, accompanied by blasts on motor-horns and voluble yelling in what was obviously highly colourful Greek. It was lucky, she thought afterwards, that she wasn't getting much sleep anyway, because sleep with that din going on all through the night would have been impossible.

Celia was sharing a room with Joan, which was quite convenient. Joan said to her as they were unpacking their bags the first day, 'Don't mind me. I shan't notice if you're here or not – and I'm a sound sleeper. I've been on too many location jobs to care where people are at night.'It was also convenient that Max had, by demand and in consequence of his status as leading actor, a room to himself. Had Celia not been on the receiving end of this piece of enforced generosity, she would have thought it typically arrogant cheek. It seemed there was a point, after all, to a film star's selfishness.

Most of the filming was taking place on the Acropolis itself, and, since the Acropolis was the major tourist attraction of the city, most of the filming had to be done early in the morning, before it was opened to the public, and late in the evening, between the daytime closing and the after-dark *Son et Lumiére* performance. In between times, filming was done on the Pnyx and Lykavitos, and down at Pireus harbour and, in order not to attract public attention, most of this filming was done on a long-distance lens

At the end of the second day's filming, Simon accosted Max in the wardrobe van with the cheerful words: 'I've got a studio set up for the dubbing. I think you should go down this evening and get it done. It's down near Syntagma – the driver knows where.'

Max groaned. 'Dubbing, after a hard day's work? And people think this is an easy life.'

Simon smiled tightly. 'Don't worry, it's only thirty loops or so.'

'Thirty loops!' Max fell back in his chair and fanned himself ostentatiously.

'And a lot of that is just grunting and groaning. I don't think there's more than ten lines of dialogue.'

'Grunting and groaning is worse than dialogue,' Max complained. 'I can never remember whether I've done an ooh or an aah, and whichever I do comes out wrong.' He hauled off his tight boots, grunting, and then said resignedly, 'Oh well, I suppose I'd better get it done. Am I to have company?'

'Yes, Chris is going to do his. You can share the car.'

'I didn't mean that, damn you,' Max said, 'as you very well knew.'

'I knew all right,' Simon agreed. 'But as it happens, Celia will be working too, so you won't be missing anything.'

'Won't I? I suppose she won't be working with you, by any chance?'

'Well, yes, as it happens,' Simon smiled, 'she'll be with me. I want to go through the rushes with her before Walter sees them. There are some things that need checking up.' His smile broadened a little at the sight of Max's discomfiture. 'So you needn't worry about her. I'll look after her all right.'

Max opened his mouth to say something, and changed his mind. He had nothing to gain at this stage by arguing with Simon. Instead he said, 'I'll go right away. You'll tell Celia where

I've gone, won't you? I think she'll be expecting me to take her to dinner.'

'Actually, she asked me to explain to you that she was working this evening. I promised I'd pass on the message,' Simon said blandly.

'Sweet little manager, aren't you?' Max said nastily. Simon nodded, and left him to it.

Simon and Celia spent two hours with their heads together over a script, going over various points that emerged from their viewing of the rushes, and then Walter arrived and they spent another hour and a half with him going through the points again. There were certain aspects of the plot which they felt hadn't emerged successfully in the filming, and a discrepancy of character which *had* emerged, and they had to decide the best way of correcting the faults without refilming more than was necessary.

'Very well,' Walter said at last. 'I think we cannot do anything more on those scenes until we have the Acropolis to ourselves. You said that it would be Saturday?'

'Saturday, yes. They're closing it to the public for the day for us,' Simon said. 'Saturday is the day most tourists are either arriving or leaving, so it was the best day for us to book the place. We'll have to share with another film company for part of the time, but I don't think that will be too much of a difficulty. Our scenes are pretty stationary.'

Walter nodded. 'And tomorrow we have the Agora?'

'That's right,' Simon said, and Celia added,

'Simon, don't forget we have to shoot there in the morning, before the sun comes round. We can't shoot facing east because of the Stoa of Attalus, which wouldn't have been there in our period.'

'Yes, of course, I had remembered,' Simon said. 'Well, if that's all, I think we had better run off and get something to eat. It's been a long day. Walter, will you join us?'

'Thank you, no, I am already engaged for the evening. I would invite you to join me, but I am dining aboard a friend's yacht.'

'That's all right,' Simon said. 'I'll look after Celia.' He put an arm round her shoulders, and she looked up at him, surprised, and then smiled. She had intended to go seeking Max as soon as she was through here, but she liked Simon, and, by the look on his face, gathered that he really wanted to dine with her. He was, after all, her boss, and it would cost her nothing to please him. She would see Max later anyway.

Dinner with Simon turned out to be more fun than she had expected. He took her to a restaurant in the richer, smarter section of the city, where the huge, new glass palaces, hotels for the American and German tourists had been built. Here they sat at a table discreetly lit with a low, heavily shaded lamp, beside a huge window with a panoramic view of the city including, inevitably, the floodlit Acropolis.

'That's one thing I don't think I could ever get tired of looking at,' Celia said when they had got to the lingering stage of their excellent meal.'It looks so improbable.I can't believe I'm actually here and looking at it. It seems far more likely that it's just a backdrop that's been lowered for the occasion.'

'I know what you mean,' Simon said. He was not looking out of the window, but at Celia. His eyes had been turned that way through most of the meal, and when she had become aware of it, kept her own eyes fixed resolutely on the view, feeling unaccountably shy. 'I felt that way the first time I saw Edinburgh Castle illuminated. It's similar in a way – it stands on a rock in the middle of a city, and at night they illuminate it, and you can't see the rock at all, only this fairy-tale castle floating in a black sky. Only there, of course, you see it from below, not above.'

'I've never been to Edinburgh,' Celia said. 'In fact, there are a lot of places I've never been to, a lot of them close to home.'

'Would you like to travel?' Simon asked her.

'Oh yes – I've always loved seeing new places. But of course, I'm in the right job now, aren't I?' She smiled, turning to look at him, and was surprised when he reached across the table and put his hand over hers.

'You are,' he said, 'if you stay in it.'

'What do you mean?' Celia asked, and her voice came out rather higher than usual.

'I think you know,' Simon said gently, his thumb caressing her hand as if he was about to hurt her and regretted the necessity. 'Celia, I'm worried about you and Max Prior. I wonder if you fully realize what you are doing.'

'I think I do,' Celia said, and her voice trembled with the effort of remaining polite, for she knew, or thought she knew, that Simon was only concerned for her in a fatherly way.

'You know, don't you, that any long-term plans would almost

114

certainly collapse. Film stars are incurably itchy-footed, and most of them, including Max, are incurably polygamous. It goes with the job. Pardon me, but the very fact that he entered so readily into an affair with you must warn you that he'd do the same with someone else the moment the opportunity arose.'

Celia strove to sound dignified and worldly-wise at the same time. 'Naturally, I know that,' she said. 'Using your own analogy, the fact that I entered into an – an affair with him – ' she paused, unsure what she was trying to say. Simon pressed her hand again.

'I don't think so,' he said. 'I hope I'm a better judge of character than that, Celia. I'm pretty sure you wouldn't have an affair with anyone you weren't very fond of. It's one of the nice things about you, but it has its disadvantages. If you were the kind of person who could carry on a casual affair without coming to any harm, I wouldn't be worried about you.'

'I don't think it's your business to be worried about me,' Celia said. 'It doesn't come into our contract – '

'I know. Please don't be angry with me. I know it's none of my business, but please believe it's a genuine regard for you that makes me say this. I only want you to be on your guard with Prior.'

'Perhaps,' Celia said, trying again for dignity, 'you don't know him as well as you think.'

There was a brief silence, and when she looked up at Simon, she saw the sadness in his face. 'Perhaps I don't,' he said at last. 'Perhaps I've misjudged him, perhaps he really has fallen in love at last. I hope so, for your sake, Celia, because anyone who marries a film actor will have a hard enough row to hoe even at that.'

'I was not aware that I mentioned marriage,' Celia said.

'No,' Simon said quietly, 'you didn't. I won't say anything more. I don't want to spoil this evening. Shall we dance? Would you like that?'

'Yes, I think I would,' Celia said. Simon stood up and pulled out her chair for her, and they walked together over to the dance-floor on the other side of the big restaurant, where four or five couples were revolving slowly to a waltz tune. With a smile, Simon held out his arms to her and Celia stepped into them, realizing for the first time what an ambiguous gesture it was. Simon's arms were pleasantly firm and warm around her, and he danced well, holding her tightly enough to guide her without squeezing her sweatily as had sometimes happened with other partners. They talked a little at first, of neutral subjects, and Simon made a few little jokes to try and lighten the atmosphere. But gradually the pleasant drug of the music and movement flowed into their veins, and they danced together in silence, their bodies moving in complete accord with each other. As she grew more relaxed and happy, Celia moved in closer to him, and without drawing attention to it, Simon drew her closer each time she yielded, until at last their bodies were pressed together and Celia's chin was resting on his shoulder, with his cheek against her hair. If she could have seen his face then, it would have explained much to her. As it was, she was aware enough to realize how lovely dancing is, how good Simon's body felt, how nice his skin smelled, and how extraordinary it was that you could embrace -and be embraced like this in a public place without it meaning anything.

It was quite late when Simon announced that they had better get back to the hotel, and Celia felt a brief pang of disappointment, for the band was still playing, the dancers were still dancing and she had wanted the delightful experience to go on indefinitely. Perhaps Simon knew a little of what she was feeling; but he was bland and polite and quite firm about it, and took her back to their hotel in a taxi without so much as holding her hand. He escorted her to her room and left her at the door with a little formal peck on the cheek.

'Good night, Celia,' he said. 'Thank you for dancing with me. Sleep well.'

Joan was in bed and asleep, and as promised, did not stir as Celia came in. She undressed and went to the bathroom and took a shower and cleaned her teeth, feeling oddly dissatisfied. Why should she *want* Simon to do more than he had done? she asked herself crossly. It would have been an impossible complication of matters, and embarrassing, and she did not want him, so why should she be disappointed that after dancing with her like that all evening he had not touched her in the taxi, or kissed her goodnight in more than that fatherly way? She was angry with herself that she should, apparently, want to ensnare Simon simply for the sake of adding his scalp to her belt. She had not thought that she was that kind of person. Simon did not think she was – he said she must be very fond of someone to have an affair with them. What was happening to her?

Perhaps it was just restlessness for Max, she decided. After all, she hadn't seen him for hours, nor made love to him for a whole day. She stepped out from under the shower, and after patting herself dry, dabbed cologne sparingly on her body, and brushed out her hair. Then she put on her chiffon and silk nightie and negligee, and, taking her room-key in her hand, slipped quietly out into the corridor. The hotel was quiet, although there were sounds in the distance – which meant that people were still up. The problem in this hotel was that if you met anyone, you couldn't pretend to be going to the bathroom. However, there could be few people in the company who did not by now know how things stood between her and Max, so what the hell. She padded quietly up the stairs and along the next floor to Max's door, and knocked quietly.

There was no answer to that or any subsequent knock. She called out softly, and put her ear to the door, but she could not hear anything, and supposed he must still be out. She was a little surprised, but then, of course, he must have had to go and get dinner after the dubbing session, and he might have been very late. She went back to her own room, took off her negligee, and lay down on the bed. She couldn't sleep. Outside the cars roared and hooted relentlessly round the square. Inside it was hot and stuffy, for the central heating was on and they had not discovered yet how to adjust it. She could not open the french windows to the balcony because the noise from the traffic would then be intolerable. All she could do was to lie still and watch the hands of her travelling-clock move round.

At two-fifteen she went again to Max's room, and still get no reply. Could he possibly be asleep? she wondered. If he was very tired from the day's filming, he might be asleep and not hear her knocking. But she wanted him badly, and he must want her too. After some indecision she went to the phone in the hall and dialled his room number, waiting half-apprehensively for him to answer. He must not be angry at being woken, she prayed. He must be glad, apologizing for falling asleep without her.

He did not answer. Impossible that he should sleep through the telephone's ringing. For one reason or another, he was not in his room. Fears and speculations raced through her. Drunk? Dead? Lost? Knocked down? Food poisoning? Images of him lying in a hospital bed, a gutter, or on a morgue slab succeeded each other in her mind. The possibility of his being in someone else's bed did not manage to force its way in with the others. She would not let it. Worried, she turned away and headed for the stairs – and came face to face with Chris Shalako.

He was bare-footed, and wearing a silk robe figured with dragons, under which he was presumably as bare as she was. His smile as he saw her was not pleasant.

'Well, well, little Celia, what are you doing here? No, don't answer that.'

'I wasn't going to,' she said shortly.

'No need, darling, I know just what's happened. Max likes to finish the night alone, does he? That's the trouble with these swollen-headed types, they give a lot of walking-home to people like you and me. Never mind, dear, we're both in the same boat. Simon's another one.'

'Another one?' Celia was puzzled.

'Who likes to spend the *rest* of the night alone, dear,' Chris said. His eyes were fixed sharply on her, and she managed in time to keep her face neutral, though not neutral enough to prevent him knowing she had understood what he was trying to imply. 'I've got a flask in my room – how about coming and sharing it with me?'

'No thanks,' Celia said, trying to pass him. He put out a hand to stop her, and anger suddenly released her tongue. 'I know what you're trying to imply,' she said, fuming, 'and I might as well say I don't believe a word of it. What I don't understand is why you're at such pains to make me believe it. First you tried to put me off Max, and now you're trying to put me off Simon. What have you to gain? I can't see it.'

Chris didn't answer her. He looked at her for a long moment, seeming not at all put out by her words, and then he said in a voice she hadn't heard him use before, a voice without any of the affectations he normally employed, 'You want to sort yourself out, Celia. But make sure you get it right. Make sure you pick the right one.' And then *he* stepped around *her*, and ran on up the stairs.

Celia made her way down to her own floor, puzzled by Chris's words and still anxious about Max; but the events of the night were not over for her yet. As she walked along the corridor to her room, a voice called her softly, and turning eagerly, thinking it was Max coming back, she saw Simon standing at the door of his room further down the corridor. He was still dressed, wearing the cords he had worn that day but with a tee-shirt. His hair was ruffled, and he looked very young and very vulnerable in the dim lighting of the passage.

'I couldn't sleep either,' he said. 'There's going to be a wonderful storm. Come and watch it with me.'

Celia hesitated for only a moment. Chris's nasty hints had aroused her protectiveness towards her boss, and to have refused him would have been to slight him, even though he would never know it. She turned and went to him, and he ushered her into his room. It was exactly like her own. The other bed in it was vacant, for it had been reserved for Bill, who was arriving on the following day. The french windows were open, and a faint breeze fluttered in, along with the undiminished roar of the traffic.

'Have some fruit juice?' he offered her. 'No ice, I'm afraid, but I've kept the tin in cold water in the bathroom. It's stifling tonight, isn't it?'

His voice was as normal as if it were an everyday thing for her to be in his room at this time of night wearing only her nightthings. He poured her a glass of orange juice, and she drank it gratefully. She had been thirsty.

'Look,' he said softly, 'the storm's beginning.' He led her to the window, and they stepped out on the balcony. 'An electric storm. They can be magnificent here. You aren't cold, are you?' Celia shook her head. 'Watch the hills,' he said.

They stood side by side at the balcony rail, and after a few seconds Celia gave a gasp of surprise as the whole sky was split with a great fork of lightning.

'Marvellous, isn't it?' Simon said.

'Aren't we in danger here?' Celia asked.

'No,' he said. 'Lightning will always take the easiest way down. There are plenty of things higher than us that would attract it if it came this way. Are you afraid?'

She glanced up at him, and relaxed suddenly. 'No, I'm not afraid,' she said. The show went on. Over the distant hills, which during the day were purple and misty on the horizon, the blue lightning forked and played, sometimes flickering like St Elmo's fires along the crests, at other times flooding the sky like a sheet of electric-blue water. It was more magnificent than anything she had ever seen; the sheer magnitude of the storm, and the power that was being unleashed, raised goose-pimples on her arms. Simon noticed them after a while, and without a word moved closer to her and put his arm round her, drawing her against him for warmth. She was not cold, but did not protest. Faced with the display of raw elementalism, she was glad of his comforting presence, warm and solid against her side. And she liked his blunt, sure hand gripping her shoulder; there was something capable and reassuring about him.

Then the thunder came, and her self-possession ceased. Idiotically, though the lightning did not worry her, the thunder made her shiver. Loud noises had always distressed her, and these thunder-claps were on a theatrical scale, almost ridiculously loud. Almost. At the first one she jumped; and at the second she shook.

'What is it?' Simon asked, looking down at her. She glanced up at his face, seeing it suddenly illuminated by a flare of blue jagged lightning. 'Are you frightened of the thunder?'

She shook her head, feeling it foolish to admit to. And then she noticed he was shaking too, trembling from his finger tips all through his strong body. Her lips parted to speak, but she had no time. 'Celia,' he said, and she was crushed to him, and his avid mouth was on hers, pouring a furious sweetness into her. For a long moment they stood there under the blazing sky, pressed together, while the thunder clattered and crashed around them as if the city were falling to pieces. Celia felt the urgency of his hard body and the hunger of his hands and lips, and wondered with a small spare piece of her mind how she could ever have thought –

It lasted for no longer than a few minutes, though it seemed to last for ages. His mouth came up from hers, he shivered and hugged her close to him, pressing her head to his chest and kissing her hair while he made wild small noises of passion and wanting, and then gently he relaxed and let her go, and when she opened her eyes and looked, bewildered, into his face, the madness had gone and there was only a questioning tenderness.

'I'm sorry,' he said gently. 'I'm sorry if I shocked you. Please forgive me. Storms seem to go to my head rather.' He gave a shaky laugh.

Celia shook her head, dazed. 'It's all right,' she said at last. 'There's nothing to forgive.'

A little while later she returned to her room, and fell asleep almost as soon as she lay down on her bed. But just before sleep overcame her, she had time to wonder why he had looked disappointed when she said that.

For the first time in weeks, Celia's first thought on waking was not for Max; it was for Simon. She remembered the strange episode of the night before, and hoped that it would not cause any change in their relationship. She would hate him to feel awkward with her, or to feel the necessity of withdrawing to a more remote position because of it. She realized how much his friendship had come to mean to her. Over the months during which she had worked for him, they had built up a marvellous relationship, frank, easy, fearless, and intimate, without any strain or tension. She hoped nothing that had happened would alter that.

Her fears were relieved as soon as she saw him at the breakfast-table: he greeted her exactly as before, except that there was perhaps the hint of a conspiratorial gleam in his eye which was certainly no change for the worse. Her mind, relieved on that point, at once returned to its other worry – full strength. Where had Max been last night? For that matter, where was he now? He had not come down to breakfast . . .

Towards the end of the meal one of the waiters brought a note to Simon. He read it with a grave little frown, then, looked up at Celia, shrugged, and handed it over as if he would have preferred not to have to do so. It was a telephone message.

'Mr Prior telephoned. He has been delayed, but will meet you on-site at nine a.m.'

So he had been out all night. The question was: where?

ELEVEN

When Max turned up at the Agora, on time, it was plain at once that wherever he had spent the night, it was not in a gutter or a hospital. He looked fresh, rested and well-fed, had bathed and shaved, and had even acquired a clean shirt from somewhere. He had evidently spent the night in some place at least as well appointed as his own hotel, and the knowledge added a fresh set of worries to those already existing in Celia's crowded mind. Moreover, she realized then that, however much she wanted to know where he had spent the night, she had no right to ask him anything.

The realization dispirited her, and, because there was nothing else that she could think of to say to him, she avoided him, keeping out of his way until he had disappeared into the clutches of Make-up and Wardrobe. Whatever he had said to her in their private moments together, however often he had told her that he loved her, she still had no claims on him (nor had he on her but that did not come into it at that point) nor any right to control or criticize his behaviour. She knew, even though she could not admit it to herself, that she wanted a long-term relationship with him, while he had never mentioned anything that could be interpreted as a long-term commitment. When they were in bed together, it was easy to believe that their love-affair would go on for ever; but when she was apart from him, it was equally easy to fear that once this film was over he would say goodbye to her without the slightest hesitation or regret.

How could she ask him? The words didn't exist in modern language, unless she talked of marriage, and she shrank from introducing such a word into their vocabulary. She supposed that was, ultimately, what she was thinking of, and yet it seemed impossibly naïve and parochial to talk of *marriage* to a famous film star, even if one was sleeping with him. *Especially* if one was sleeping with him.

It was easy enough to keep out of his way while the filming was going on, and to disappear on messages in the pauses between takes. In any case, the filming was going on at full speed, as always with a small, budget-conscious company, and Max's attention was wholly engrossed with Walter's directions. But once the sun had come round and the cameras were facing into it, the filming had to stop, and Max came straight away, before he had even changed and taken off his make-up, to find her.

'Ah, there you are,' he said, catching her by the elbow and turning her round to face him. He was staring at her keenly and not in an entirely friendly way. 'How lovely you are looking today. I like that hat – it matches the colour of your hair.'

Celia had thought she *was* looking well – her velvet-cord suit was sage-green, and with it she wore a silk shirt of pale *eau-de-nil* colour open low in the neck to show off her sun-tan, and a broad-brimmed straw hat trimmed with pale green ribbons – but Max's tone of voice seemed to imply something unpleasant and sinister about her looks. She faced up to him gravely. 'It was meant to,' she said.

'And did you enjoy your little jaunt last night?' he asked her. 'I hope you didn't catch cold running about the hotel with nothing on.'

'I can guess who told you that,' she said. 'Christopher seems to make a living telling tales about other people.'

Max shrugged. 'So what, if they're true. You don't deny you *were* wandering about last night, do you?'

She looked at him sadly. 'I was thinking when you arrived this morning how I don't have any right to ask you where you were last night. It made me feel sad. That was why I didn't come and speak to you.'

He had the grace to look a little ashamed. 'You're right,' he said. 'You don't have any right. And I don't have any right to ask you. But all the same – I can't help feeling jealous. Simon has all the breaks. He can command you whenever he wants. You should feel flattered that I get jealous about you.'

'I don't think jealousy is a compliment. I'm glad you care about me enough to care what I do, if that's what you mean. But actually I was out of my room last night looking for you. I went to your room, and met Chris on the way back. That was all.' She would not tell him about the visit to Simon's room. Not unless she had to. That was private to Simon.

Max smiled suddenly, his teeth showing very white against his made-up face. 'Was that really all?' he said. 'Oh, I'm so glad. I've been in a perfect ferment. I had no right to ask you – I'm sorry. Forgive me.'

She was a little puzzled. 'You didn't ask me,' she said. 'I told you.' She waited, but still he did not tell her where he had been. She opened her mouth to ask him, and shut it again. No, let her at least be true to her own standards. Perhaps he would tell her later.

'I'm going to get changed and cleaned up,' he said without acknowledging her remark. 'I'll be as quick as I can. Wait for me, and I'll take you for a walk through the flea market. You've never been there, have you?'

'No,' she said.

'Good. I'd like you to go for the first time with me. Don't get caught up with Simon again, will you? I won't be long.'

He ran off towards the wardrobe van, and Celia shrugged slightly and went to find Simon. Whatever Max said, she was only there to do a job, and she must get clearance from Simon before she went off on a pleasure jaunt. Simon made no objection, however. He smiled pleasantly, and said, 'Of course, go and enjoy yourself. I'm going to do a bit of sightseeing myself. We can go through some things later this afternoon, when you get back to the hotel. Say around six-thirty?'

'Yes, all right. I'll make sure I'm back by then. Thanks Simon.'

'Don't mention it. Have a nice time,' he said.

She left him, wondering at his change of attitude. Yesterday he seemed to want to separate her from Max, and today he was positively encouraging her to spend time with him. Was he, perhaps, hoping for a petard hoist job?

The flea market was only a hop, step and jump from the Agora, and a very short time later Celia and Max were walking under the banner at the entrance and moving slowly down the narrow street, staring at the heaped goods inside and outside the shops on either side of them.

'For tourist junk, it's very good,' Max said.' Look at this brass stuff, for instance. You couldn't get anything anywhere near that price at home.'

He went over and picked up various things – candlesticks and fire-irons and inkwells, and the fat, smiling proprietor at once appeared in the doorway saying, 'Please. Come in. Lovely things inside. Come in, see inside.'

Max ignored him as if he were not there; Celia thought this

rather rude, and in mitigation smiled at the man and shook her head. It at once appeared that this was a mistake, for, encouraged, the man stepped down, put a hand on her shoulder, and, still smiling, began to urge her towards the door.

'Please. Yes. Inside, much more things. What you want? Brasses, horse brasses, very nice? Fry-pans, cooking-pots, all copper, lovely. You come inside, just see.'

'No, no thank you, I don't want any today,' Celia muttered, embarrassed. Max glanced up, grinning, and shot something in rapid Greek at the man, who relinquished his hold on her with a shrug and went back to his doorway, still watching them with the speculative eye of a temporarily defeated hyena.

Max put an arm round Celia and they walked on. 'Don't look at them or speak to them, that's the rule. They don't mean any harm, but they don't give up easily, and a soft touch like you will end up loaded down with junk unless you learn to harden your tender heart and ignore them,' Max said. 'Look at those sheepskins. Do you know how much they cost in England? And leather, my God! And, you know, they think they're rooking us!'

The leather and sheepskin shop delayed them for some time, and when they finally emerged into the sunshine, Celia was carrying a beautiful tan leather shoulder-bag which Max had bought for her for the equivalent of five pounds. Celia knew for a fact that it would have cost at least double that in England, and she would have bought it for herself had he not forestalled her. Such bargains were all around them, and their progress up the street was slow.

They came to the road junction at the halfway point, and there Celia stopped with a little cry to watch a young man with the curly hair of a faun who was selling string-puppets. 'Oh look,' she said, remembering in time to say it quietly. The young man appeared totally absorbed in his demonstration. The puppet he was handling was a crudely-shaped representation of an ostrich, with long bendy legs and neck and huge feet, and he managed it with a skill that transformed it magically into a living character. There was a rudimentary pavement at that point in the street, and the ostrich walked up to the kerb and stretched its neck, inspecting the slight step upwards with interest, tilting its head to view it sideways in a most bird-like way. Then, one huge foot at a time, it scaled the step as if it were a monstrous height. Gaining the top, the bird gave a little skip and a quick, dabbing

125

preen at its sides, as if hugely pleased with itself, and then turned round, manoeuvering its feet with the exagegrated care of one who is forever treading on one with the other, teetered on the edge for a moment, and then gave a huge, clumsy leap back down into the gutter, overbalanced, tripped on its own toes, and sat down heavily.

Celia laughed aloud, delightedly, and the young man looked up shyly from under his eyelashes, smiled with pleasure at her approbation and, without attempting to apply any sales pressure, began a new performance.

'Isn't he good?' Celia said, turning to Max – only to find he was not there. She looked up the street and down, wondering where he had got to – evidently he had not stopped when she had. She could not see him anywhere, and for a moment she considered going on and looking for him, and then decided that he would come back for her as soon as he realized she was not with him. She wanted to watch the puppeteer for a little longer – already he had walked his bird over to the box containing the rest of his stock and was putting it through a pantomime of trying to wake them up and trying to climb into the box.

Celia watched, and from time to time glanced up the street for Max. She was just getting to the point where she felt she had to buy one of these delightful puppets, despite the fact she had no one to give it to and no one to perform with it before, when, looking back down the street she caught a glimpse through the meandering crowds of Max's back. He was talking to someone who was partly obscured by his body, talking fairly earnestly, by the movement of his shoulders and the occasional wave of a hand. A shopkeeper? No. As he moved slightly she saw that it was a woman, too smartly dressed to be a local. Celia couldn't see her face from where she stood, and hesitatingly she began to move towards them, some instinct keeping her to the side of the street and concealed by the shoppers.

With a final large gesture, Max seemed to finish his conversation, and turned away, giving Celia a full view of the woman. She was small and slender, very smartly dressed in a beige trouser-suit; thick corn-coloured hair, lots of gold jewellery, large lizard handbag, huge sunglasses that almost obscured a face that was just faintly familiar to Celia. The woman stared after Max, and then gave a tiny shrug and turned away, walking rapidly back the way they had come. Celia quickly turned also and pretended to examine a jewellers' shop window, not wanting Max to know she had seen him talking. She would give him the chance to tell her. If he did, it would prove that there was nothing suspicious in it. Who on earth could she be? It wasn't anyone from their company, and by her clothes she must be a tourist or visitor of some sort to the city. Of course, people did go there on holiday, and it was quite possible for someone like Max, who must have a large acquaintance, to meet an old friend.

But the conversation had not looked like the usual goodness-fancy-meeting-you-here what-are-you-up-to-these-days chat that one would exchange on meeting an old friend unexpectedly. It looked somehow more serious. Well, let him tell her. If he met an acquaintance by accident he would surely tell her. Her heart hammering, she waited for him to find her. Her eyes were fixed almost glassily on the window, and after a breathless pause the reflection of Max's face came up beside hers in the dark glass, and his hand came down on her shoulder.

'There you are,' he said. He peered over her shoulder, and she noticed his breath coming a little hard for someone who had done no more than stroll slowly along a flat street. 'Let me see if I can guess.'

'Guess what?' Celia asked. Her voice sounded suspiciously squeaky to her, but he didn't seem to notice.

'What it is you're staring at like a cat at a canary. Hm, hm, not bangles, nor ear-rings, I fancy. Not those nasty great rings. No, no, no – ah! That must be it. Yes, definitely.' He paused, but could not tempt her curiosity. He had to ask himself. 'I know what it is – the only thing in the window fit to touch any part of you. Shall we go in and buy it?'

She turned then to look up at him, wondering what new deception was to be practised on her, and saw that he had put on his sunglasses. His eyes were almost invisible behind the dark lenses. so she couldn't see his expression.

'What a deep and earnest look, my darling,' he said. She looked at him imploringly, but she was staring at a shuttered house.

'Tell me,' she begged.

There was a brief silence, and for a moment she thought the communication was about to come; but he smiled lightly and said, 'Why, *that*, of course,' and pointed to something in the window. Had he not understood her plea? Or, understanding,

127

had he chosen to ignore it? She would never know. She turned away to the window again, and saw nothing that was there.

'I'm going to buy it for you,' he said. 'Stay here – this time you mustn't know how much I'm spending on you.'

A few moments later he was back, to find her still staring blankly ahead.

'There,' he said. 'I'll put it on you. I'm glad you didn't come in. It cost a lot more than I thought it would, you see, and you might have been forced to witness my hesitations. Parsimony is not a pretty sight.' While he talked he stepped round behind her, and a moment later she felt him place something round her neck and fix the clasp behind. 'It looks beautiful,' he said, kissing the back of her neck before he let her long hair fall back into place. 'Just about beautiful enough for you.'

She looked down, her hand wandering up blindly to touch it. When her sight cleared, she saw that it was indeed beautiful. Her fingers closed round it. It was a little dolphin, carved out of a piece of jade, arching his back in a leap, and hanging by a tiny ring from a thin gold chain.

'Dolphins are lucky,' Max said. 'And they're specially favoured in Greece. He'll bring you luck.'

'Thank you,' she said in a muted voice. He turned her round abruptly and took her in his arms, hugging her fiercely as if he was about to be parted from her, and she felt in his touch all the layers upon layers of mutual knowledge and deception. She returned his embrace. He would tell her when he could. Despite all seeming, he loved her. 'Thank you,' she said again, but more heartily this time. 'It really is beautiful. I shall always treasure it.'

He released her, and they walked on down the street, their arms wound round each other, silent, but in accord.

Simon bent his head to examine it, and then stepping back said, 'You're very lucky. I should think it's quite valuable. As far as I can see, it's flawless, and a very good piece of jade.'

'Is jade valuable, then?' Celia asked. 'I always thought of it as a semi-precious stone.'

'Good jade is very valuable,' Simon said. 'I'd be surprised if Max didn't pay two or three hundred for that.'

Celia paled slightly. 'Not really?'

'Did I shock you? Sorry. I should have it valued when you get back to England. You might want to have it insured. It really is a very pretty piece, anyway.'

'It's for luck,' Celia said vaguely. She hadn't imagined he had paid anything like that amount for the dolphin. She had been thinking of somewhere about the twenty-pound mark, and would have thought that a generous present to buy someone on the spur of the moment. She had to convince herself it was a lucky charm, or she wouldn't have the nerve to wear it.

She and Simon were engaged in their evening work and it was nearing dinner-time.

'I'm going out to the airport to meet Bill after this, and we'll be getting a bite to eat somewhere. Will you join us?' Simon asked. Celia looked doubtful. She hadn't actually arranged anything with Max, but she expected they would be eating together. Simon read her hesitation, and said, 'It's all right. Just a thought. Not to worry.'

'Thanks, Simon, but –'

'It's all right,' he repeated, with a reassuring smile. 'I understand perfectly.'

Which is more than I do, Celia thought to herself. They finished their work, and Simon took himself off to collect Bill, while Celia went back to her room to shower and change and wait for Max to call for her. It was getting quite late, and she was hungry. Once she was ready, she wandered about the room a little, restlessly, and then went out on to the balcony and leaned on the rail, staring out over the city. It was lovely at this time of night, when the dusk was drawing on and the lights were beginning to twinkle here and there. The sky was a plummy red over the mountains, but still a pale, clear blue overhead. The traffic honked and roared – she had gotten to the stage where she almost didn't notice it.

Glancing down, she caught a glimpse of someone going round the corner towards the hotel entrance, and was sure it was Max. Her excitement rose up in her again. He would be here any moment. She went back inside and put on a dab more perfume, and visualized him – now he would be standing by the lifts, now he would be going up in one, now he would be stepping out and walking along the passage, now he would be putting his hand up to knock –

She had got him up to her door four times before the knock came, and she flew to answer it – and found one of the hotel clerks standing there with a note in his hand.

Doom, despair. She managed to thank the clerk and send him away. Notes had to be bad news. Or perhaps it was from Max, suggesting a rendezvous? But no, if that were so, he would have come up, or phoned her. She opened the note and read it, and then screwed up the paper and threw it with an angry gesture at the wastepaper-bin. And missed it, of course.

He had to go out on business. He was sorry he couldn't have dinner with her. He hoped he might be able to join her later.

She took off the pink silk jersey dress she had put on especially for him and hung it up in the wardrobe again. Too smart for anything but a special dinner with Max. She had turned down dinner with Simon and Bill, which would have been fun, for *this*. It was almost too late to get dinner anyway. She couldn't go out into the streets alone, not here, not being blonde. She would have to take the hotel dinner, and she'd have to be quick to get even that. Anger and disappointment. She felt tears behind her eyes, and pressed her fingers over her eyelids to force them back. Business. What business? The blonde woman? Damn, damn, damn. Why did she have to feel like this? Why did she have to care?

Trust him, or stop caring, she told herself angrily. She put on a pair of trousers and a cheesecloth shirt, dabbed cold water on her face to soothe it, picked up her handbag and key, and went out, making her way down the stairs to the hotel dining-room. The waiter greeted her and escorted her to a seat with an expression of silent sympathy, mixed with the kind of lascivious calculation with which male hotel staff abroad eye the lone female tourist. It is well known that English females go abroad purely in order to get themselves screwed. They can't do it at home, poor creatures - too inhibited - and besides, English men are poor, cold lovers. No wonder the women flock to the warm countries where a man knows how to take a woman. A rapid, sidelong glance ascertained her room number; now he had only to watch for the signs. There were any number of them, but one way or another the invitation always came. One must be discreet.

The hotel dinner was plain and dull and curiously stateless – it would have been impossible to tell the country of origin of any part of that meal, had one not known where one was. Celia ate it without noticing. She had been hungry, and the food filled her. That was all there was to the meal, until she got to the dessert stage, when her evening was saved from ruin by the entry of Simon and Bill. They spotted her straight away, and came and joined her at her table.

'We thought it was getting late so we decided to come back and feed at the hotel trough,' Bill said when he had greeted and kissed Celia. 'It's lovely to see you again – and what luck, bumping into you like this.'

'I am staying here,' Celia said drily, and Bill laughed off the gaffe.

'What's the grub like? Awful?'

'Oh – all right, I suppose,' Celia said, glancing down in surprise at her plate as if she had not realized until then that she was eating. Simon noticed this, as he noticed everything, and he looked at her with sympathy, but said nothing, for which Celia was grateful.

'Will you stay and talk to us while we eat?' he asked her. 'And then, if you haven't anything else to do, we could take you for a moonlit look at the Plaka – that's the old sector of the city, very quaint and romantic. Bill has a fancy to see it.' Bill shot Simon a look which said *oh have I?* but he backed him up loyally.

'Yes, the first thing I want to do every time I come to Athens is to go and look at the Plaka. I can never quite believe it exists.'

Celia lingered over her coffee while the two men made short work of their meal. Despite the wording of Simon's invitation, she did very little of the talking, but by the time they were ready to leave, she was much more relaxed and happy, and was smiling at some of the things Bill said, and contributing the occasional remark. Bill and Simon had worked together for long enough to be able to put up a very solid front when necessary; and both had worked with Celia for long enough to make it very difficult for her not to feel at one with either or both of them.

A taxi took them to the Plaka, and Celia found that it was, as Bill said, unbelievable, and would have been just as much so by daylight. The old sector of the city clung to the sides of the Acropolis hill, and the houses were tiny and flat-roofed and painted all different colours, lemon and rose and white, peach and sky-blue and sage-green, geranium-red, brick-pink, shrieking mauve and chocolate. The hill was so steep that the roads that led up were interspersed with flights of steps, short and long, cut out of the rock itself, and the houses were frequently on two or three levels each; the tiny roads, often no more than three feet wide, ducked and twisted in and out of the dwellings, presenting a jumbled view of doors and windows and roofs, the roof of one house adjoining the doorstep of another. From unbelievably tiny spaces trees poked up their fragile branches, and there were flowers everywhere, blooming wherever they could find room, and massed in any receptacle that would hold sufficient earth.

It was a magical, fairy-tale place – Celia practically expected the seven dwarfs to tramp out of one of the tiny dwellings – and over it all brooded the ancient and beautiful temple that stood out starkly floodlit against the sky at the top of the rugged rock to which the houses clung. Reaching the top of the walk and the level path that runs around the rock just below the summit, they stopped to look back down over the jumbled, moon-shadowed roofs and beyond over the great city that filled the entire basin within the ring of hills.

'Thank you for bringing me,' she said to the two men, who stood one on either side of her like protective angels. 'You were right, it is a wonderful sight. I'm glad I didn't miss it.'

'Let's walk down and have a quick look at the Roman Agora,' Bill suggested. 'It's right in our way.'

'We were there today,' Celia said.

'No, that's the Agora,' Simon corrected her. 'The Roman Agora's a different place. You'll see. And then we'll go and get some coffee somewhere, shall we? And have a nice cosy chat together. We've got a lot to discuss.'

They walked back down the hill, and after a short walk came to the wide open square in which the remains of the Roman Agora stood, again floodlit, and surrounded by shady walks between trees and aromatic shrubs. After admiring the tall, fluted columns, the three of them made their way by one of these winding walks towards the edge of the square nearest home, where they hoped to pick up a taxi. It was obviously a favourite place for lovers, for in every nook and grotto there was a bench on which shadowy figures embraced, ignoring the passing walkers who were probably more embarrassed than the lovers.

'Well, it isn't what it was built for,' Bill said cheerfully, 'but I dare say the Romans would be happy that it's still being used. They were a very practical people, the Romans.'

He was leading the way along a narrow path that wound in and out of bushes and small clumps of trees, and as he turned a corner he stopped abruptly, and turned, almost bumping into

132

Celia, who was behind him.

'I think this is the wrong way,' he said. 'I think we should go that way.' But he wasn't quick enough to prevent either of his companions seeing the couple who sat on a bench a little way ahead, clearly defined in the mixture of moon-and floodlight. The man was Max, and the woman was the smart blonde woman he had spoken to in the flea market earlier that day. They were sitting close together engaged in what was obviously a very absorbing conversation, and she was holding one of his hands.

The three of them about-turned and headed along another path until they came out into the open by the triumphal arch. Simon looked gravely at Celia, and she avoided his eyes, but felt she must say something, to show she was not completely stricken.

'It's a funny thing about being blonde,' she said lightly, 'but one never minds much being passed over for a brunette or a red-head; but when it's another blonde, one feels betrayed.'

'Perhaps it isn't what you think,' Simon said gently. Bill shot him an astonished glance, his eyebrows climbing his forehead, and Simon shook his head slightly at his companion. Celia looked up just too late to catch the exchange.

'What do you mean?'

'You don't know who that was? It was August Dane.'

The film star – so that was why she looked vaguely familiar to Celia. Had she not been wearing those huge glasses, Celia would have known her at once.

'August Dane?' she repeated on a slightly querying note.

'Max Prior's ex-wife,' Simon said.

'Oh,' Celia said. They took a taxi back to the hotel, and went to the bar there for their coffee.

TWELVE

The coffee-shop and bar stayed open until the small hours for the convenience of the hotel guests, but at a little after one Celia tired of sitting and talking as if nothing had happened, and excused herself. Simon and Bill remained talking and finishing their drinks and Celia made her way out, intending to go up to bed; but as she turned the corner towards the stairs, she was accosted by Max, coming up the stairs from the ground floor.

'Oh, *there* you are,' he said as if he had been searching all over the place for her. He caught her arm clumsily, pinching it so that she snatched it back with a small cry. He smelled of drink, and she pulled back from him a little. He noticed the gesture and straightened himself and addressed her coolly: 'No, I'm not drunk,' he said. 'I have had a few drinks, but I'm not by any means drunk. Come with me. I want to talk to you.'

She regarded him steadily, and he met her eyes without hesitation. She read in his face the knowledge that she knew where he had been and with whom. In those circumstances, it seemed reasonable to comply. She turned and walked beside him, and they mounted the stairs to his room, without his making any attempt to touch her, or speaking a word, until they were safely inside his room. He switched on the small lamp over the bed, which gave a soft light to the room, and then turned and simply held out his arms to her.

Her hesitation was no more than momentary. Seconds later she was hugging him, and being hugged by him, and their mouths were anxiously seeking each other out. There seemed to be no point in talking then. They undressed and lay down on the bed and made love with the clean simplicity of two animals, finding a harmony through their bodies that they couldn't find in speech.

Afterwards, he rolled on to his back and drew her against him, settling her head on his shoulder, stroking her hair and kissing her brow with a happy sigh.

'You've got an arm like a bunch of rocks,' Celia said at last. 'Don't you like it?'

'I wasn't complaining.' Close-up, his face looked tired. The lines that during the day dissolved themselves in his general animation showed up sharply in repose. She supposed he must be around forty years old. She knew so little about him. His eyes were closed now, the soft fans of lashes brushing his cheek, the lines running away three ways from the outer corners of the lids. She didn't want him to fall asleep. She felt relaxed, unthreatened.

'Was that where you were last night?' she said.

He grunted interrogatively, and then his eyes opened and he peered down at her as if to see what her mood was. 'I thought you decided for yourself that you had no right to ask questions?' he said. He didn't sound angry.

'I did,' she said. 'I haven't any *right*, but I'm asking them all the same. You don't have to answer.'

He considered this. 'Yes, that was where I was. But it was not, perhaps, what you might think. I went to see her, at her hotel. It got very late, and I'd drunk rather a lot, and when she suggested I stay the night, I did. In a spare bed.'

Celia tried to shrug, which was difficult in a lying down position. 'It isn't my business what you do,' she began, but he pressed her tighter against him to stop her.

'It is. Don't speak like that. She's nothing to me any more. I didn't go there to screw her. I know you didn't ask, but I'm telling you that. A free gift. Darling, Celia, believe me. Believe I love you.'

'If you don't care for her, why do you go and see her?' she asked in a small voice, willing to be reassured. 'And why the secrecy?'

'I was afraid you wouldn't understand. I'm still afraid you won't. You've never been married, so how can you know what it's like? When you've been married to a person, shared a home with them, lived with them for years, shared all your thoughts, everything – however much you may come to dislike them, however little you love them, you can't just turn off every feeling, just like that. You still *care* about them, in the sense that you care what happens to them. It's like a relative – a brother or sister. Even if you hate them, they're still your brother or sister. You can't change a fact.'

'You should have explained it to me,' Celia said reproachfully. 'You didn't give me a chance.'

135

'Well, I've told you now. Let's not talk about it any more. Kiss me again – I haven't tasted you for so long, I've almost forgotten what you taste like.'

There were a lot more things she wanted to say and to ask – she would have liked to have a long talk with him, but he silenced her with kisses, and then their familiar response to each other's bodies prevented any more speech.

'You'll kill me in the end,' he said sleepily, a long time afterwards. 'I've never known anyone like you – I just can't keep my hands off you. Darling – Celia.' His voice distorted with a yawn. 'Can't get enough – of you.' And very shortly he was asleep. Celia was only moments behind him. She was in the middle of thinking that if she didn't get up and go back to her own room she would fall asleep; and the next thing she knew the phone was ringing with Max's early morning call, and she had to scramble into her clothes and dash off to her own room before the maid arrived with the tea-tray. By the time Joan woke up with her own alarm, Celia was already under the shower and singing.

Despite the fact that it had been closed to the public, the Acropolis seemed very crowded that morning, with two film crews wandering about it. The other film company seemed to have a large number of extras, and it was only by virtue of the period costumes that Celia was able to pick out her own extras, who were her particular responsibility, at a distance. Simon and Walter were already deep in conversation with their opposite numbers in the other company, deciding who should have what and when, and the gaffer, a brawny, balding man with a foghorn voice, had pinned Celia against the wall with a list of complaints about the lack of facilities and the interference he was already suffering from the presence of the rivals.

The needs of the two films, however, were not really conflicting, and everything was soon sorted out satisfactorily. Satisfactorily from the professional point of view, Celia thought – from her own point of view she was distressed to see that this was the company which supplied the reason for August Dane's presence in Athens. She was very much in evidence, walking about and giving orders in a loud, rather piercing voice. She was not only ACC Studios' hottest cinematographic property, but she was also a not unimportant shareholder, and was thus able to use a great deal of influence to get things done the way she liked them. Even the director looked slightly cowed before her, and directors are normally the most autocratic members of the film-making team.

She looked pretty good, too, in her costume and make-up, with her corn-gold hair bouncing round her shoulders. Every few minutes a dresser would run up and rearrange a curl, never disturbing August Dane's stride as she did so. It was a set-up that made Bantham Films look like a university group, except for the presence of such eminently successful people as Walter Bruno, Christopher Shalako and Maxwell Prior.

Perhaps it was the presence of his ex-wife on the site, or his lack of sleep, or too much to drink the night before, but whatever the cause, Max took it into his head to be difficult that morning, and Celia was called in twice, once by Wardrobe and once by Make-up, to sort things out and sooth ruffled feelings. She had the feeling that he was doing it deliberately to provoke her, but she would not play on their private relationship in public – it would have been unprofessional. She spoke to him exactly as she would have spoken to any actor in the same situation, and if he seemed piqued that she would not lovey-dovey him out of his ill-temper, she feigned not to notice it.

Once the filming started, *his* professionalism took over, and he worked hard and uncomplainingly despite the heat, the heavy, prickly costumes, and the sweat which made it necessary continually to retouch his make-up. The filming did not go particularly well. He and Chris had to have a fight in this scene, and they had to do it three times before they got it right, which was hot and exhausting for them both; and then Fern, who had to intervene in the fight and try to stop them, slipped on the edge of the temple steps and turned her ankle, which instantly swelled up and caused her great pain. Joan and Celia did the best they could for her with a cold-water bandage, and when she had rested it for ten minutes she bravely decided to go on. Celia privately doubted whether she could walk on it without either showing the pain or favouring it, but to her eternal credit she got through the rest of the filming without giving a sign of it, sitting down between takes and massaging her ankle with her face puckered ruefully.

Celia was kept pretty busy running backwards and forwards warding extras and service crew members from ACC's side of the site out of the line of filming, and this was a job, in the prevailing heat, and added to all her other normal tasks, that she could have done without. It was while doing this that she caught a glimpse from time to time of August Dane in her floating chiffon dress acting out her part with her handsome, grey-haired lead man, Paul Newson. Celia was always too far away to judge what kind of a performance she was putting up, but she certainly looked very impressive.

Because they only had the one full day's filming, Simon and Walter had gone to the expense and trouble of setting up a monitor screen on site so that they could view roughly what was being shot without having to wait for the rushes which, of course, they would not have been able to view until the late afternoon at the soonest. It was as well that they did, because it turned out to be quite a job preventing the background of modern Athens from creeping into the shots as the camera followed the action, and without the help of the monitor they would almost certainly have had to throw out quite a lot of the day's takes. They finished at last, however, at almost the same time as the ACC crowd, and the site rang with the shouts of the crews taking down and packing up their equipment, and the chatter of the actors and extras as they waited their turns to use the overcrowded vans. Chris and Fern had not been used in the last shots, and they had taken the opportunity to get in quickly and change, and gone off to visit the ACC people on the other side of the hill. Max had just finished changing and was taking off his make-up and talking to Celia when they returned, accompanied by August Dane and Paul Newson.

'Hello darling,' August Dane greeted her ex-husband. He looked past Celia with a forbidding expression. 'How cross you look – it must be the heat.'

'Hello Gussie,' he said unenthusiastically. 'Had a good day?'

'As well as can be expected. I loathe location work, as *you* well know.' Her voice was loaded with secrets. 'And all that stand-ing's murder for poor Paul, isn't it, Paul darling?' Paul darling looked sheepish, as if he wished she wouldn't, but she went on anyway. 'It's his veins, poor sweetheart. Still, only another week to go, and then it's back to dear old England for a while. You're going back too, aren't you, darling?'

'Next week,' Max said non-committally.

'Well, maybe we'll travel together. Anyway, what we came to ask you was if you'll have dinner with Paul and me. Chris is coming, and Fern's joining us later when she's rested her leg, poor precious.' She flashed a glittering smile at Fern, who smirked back awkwardly like a small sugar-mouse. 'So we only need you to make the party *perfect*.'

'Well, thanks all the same, Gussie, but I was actually – ' his voice petered out as he glanced at Celia. August Dane glanced at Celia too, and gave a minutely different smile from the one she gave Fern.

'Oh yes, this is your new little friend, isn't it? But I'm sure Miss – Er – will let you off for tonight – for an *old friend*. And we have so little time together nowadays.'

Celia felt herself swelling with venom, like a snake, but she would not allow herself to be outfaced by this monster of a woman. With icy calm she said, 'That's quite all right, Miss Dane. It wasn't a definite engagement. Max is perfectly free as far as I'm concerned.'

'Super. How kind,' August Dane said. 'Well, Maxie darling, what do you say?'

Paul Newson meanwhile was looking slightly put-out, and he intervened at that moment out of sheer kindness. 'Why shouldn't she – Miss Um – why not join us? It would make the numbers even. Would you perhaps join us for dinner?' he appealed to Celia, and she gave him a smile in recognition of his better manners and kind intentions.

'No, really,' she said, 'thank you, but I'm rather tired. I think I'll have an early night.'

'Celia – ' Max began, but when she looked at him she saw that he would go – either because he had to, or because he wanted to.

'That's all right, Max,' August Dane said. 'I'm sure she knows her own mind. Now hurry up and get ready, and we'll take you back to our hotel in our car. You can change there – I'm sure we've got enough of your clothes for you to choose something. Come along, you two – we'll wait for you at the car, Max.'

She sailed off with Paul Newson and Fern at her heels, and Celia, not wishing to wait and hear anything Max might have to say, stumbled off blindly in the other direction, only to come face to face with Chris Shalako, who had doubled back to meet her.

'You did it deliberately,' Celia said. 'You arranged it.' He didn't deny her charge.

'That'll fix you, you money-grubbing little bitch!' he hissed at her. She recoiled in shock from the unexpected venom.

'What – ?' she began feebly.

'And you'll find there's plenty I can do that I haven't done yet, if you mess Simon around.'

'What are you talking about? What have I ever done to you? Why are you doing this to me?' Celia was bewildered even more than hurt. Chris's face tightened up with some unnameable anguish. He even clenched his fists, not threateningly, but as if he were having a job to force the words out.

'I can't stand seeing a great bloke like Simon mixed up with a gold-digging tart like you,' he said, 'but if you're what he wants – ' His eyes narrowed. 'But I warn you, if you mess him around – '

'Simon?' she said faintly. She wondered if she weré going mad. 'What's that got to do with Max and – that woman?'

'He always goes back to her, you know, 'Chris said as if she hadn't spoken. 'About every six months on average. He never wanted the divorce – it was her. He can't let her alone. You might as well get your claws out of him, because he won't marry you. You'll never get a penny out of him. He'll sleep with her tonight, just like last night, and every night she wants him. She only has to crook her finger. So now you know.'

And with that he was gone, sprinting away over the uneven ground like a vandal fleeing the scene of his crime. Celia stood there trembling, unable to make sense of what had happened, but unable to keep out the hurt all the same.

She stayed where she was for a long time, until she had stopped trembling. When she got back, Max had gone, and Simon was looking for her. He took her arm and drew her aside to a quiet corner.

'Celia, are you all right?' he asked anxiously. 'I saw that woman come over – did she make trouble?' Celia looked up at him, unable to speak, hoping he would understand from her expression. He bit his lip with a troubled frown, and then took her hands in his and chafed them. 'Don't take it too much to heart, Celia,' he said. 'She's a prize bitch, but you should really feel sorry for someone like her. She's so insecure she has to be rude to everyone to build herself up in her own eyes.'

'I didn't mind her,' she said at last. 'I'm just – confused.'

'I expect you are. Come on, we've got work to do – that will take your mind off things. Look, are you – is he – Max, I mean – '

'Max has gone with her. They're dining together,' she said expressionlessly.

140

'Oh.' He looked at her with acute sympathy. 'Oh Celia. I'm sorry.' She roused herself.

'Don't be,' she said. 'It wasn't as serious as you thought. I was never in danger from him, you know.'

It was a big lie, and perhaps Simon knew it as well as she did. 'Do you want to go back to England?' he asked. 'Bill is going tomorrow night, you can go back with him.'

'What about the work here?'

'I can manage.'

'No,' she said at last. 'I won't go. Thanks, but it would be unprofessional.'

Admiration lit his face, and something else – relief? 'Good girl,' he said. 'I'm glad you feel that way. I was afraid you'd want to leave altogether. Leave Bantham, I mean.'

She smiled slightly. 'I begin to get the picture.' He had been worried all along that she would have a bad affair with Max, and walk out of the job, leaving him, Simon, with an unfinished film and no assistant. Well, it might have happened before; it was the classic objection to employing women; but it would not happen with her. 'Don't worry, Simon, I won't let you down.'

'Look,' he said as they walked back. 'Tomorrow is Sunday. Rest-day for the actors. We'll have some work to do in the morning, but in the afternoon, how about taking a trip out somewhere? It's too hot to stay in Athens. We might get a boat and go and look at one of the islands?'

'Just you and me?' she asked. He looked worried. 'Well, yes, that was what I meant. But if you don't like it –'

'Oh, I like it,' she said. But will Chris Shalako like it? But she didn't say that aloud. There was still something she didn't understand, and now was not the time for stirring up trouble.

Celia was down for breakfast very early the next morning, but she was not the first. Max was there, sitting alone at a table with coffee before him, dressed, washed and shaved, looking as if he had been up for hours, or as if he had never been to bed. He looked up quickly as she came in, and leaned over to pull out the chair next to him, as a sign that she should sit with him. She did not hesitate. She had the feeling that he had been waiting for her, though whether he had come to the breakfast table from his own hotel room or his ex-wife's she did not know, would probably never know. There was unfinished business between them, even she recognized that.

She sat down on the offered chair, and ordered her breakfast from the waiter who drifted up with perfect timing. She was aware of Max's eyes on her, and she trembled, though she tried not to show it. *You can't just turn off your feelings*, she thought. She still desired him – loved him, if love was what she had felt for him in these past weeks. What she had shared with him had been very real, and in a sense they belonged to each other in some small way because of it, and always would. It was just a fact.

'Celia,' he began, and she looked at him then, at the face she knew, had loved, cared for still. But she didn't feel the same, she realized at once. He was not hers. That made a difference. 'I'm sorry '

'Please don't apologize,' she said, meaning it sincerely 'I understand, Max. Perhaps better than you think. We had fun together, and it's over. I don't bear you any ill-will. Quite the contrary.'

'You're so calm about it,' he said, seeming surprised and perhaps a little hurt. 'I didn't expect you to be calm. I behaved very badly. I shouldn't have let her speak to you like that. It won't happen again. I was – I don't know – sort of *blitzed*, I suppose. She has that effect on me.' He reached out to take her hand, and she let him. She felt friendly towards him, though underneath there was a kind of hurt she did not yet understand. 'Anyway, we're leaving soon, and she's staying on here for another week, so I won't be seeing her.'

She realized suddenly that he was thinking they would go on as they had been before. Carefully, she chose the words to disabuse him. 'Max, I really meant it.'

'Meant it?' He screwed up his eyes in puzzled amusement. 'Meant what?'

'That it's over.' The words sounded ridiculously trite, but what else could she say.

'I don't understand,' he said flatly.

'I think you do. I never had the right to ask you anything. You said I was your present, and I'd have settled for that. Even without anything said about the future. But I suppose I'm hopelessly old-fashioned, or something, but I won't share you with anyone. While it's me, it's got to be me only. And since I see now that it can't be me only, I have to say – ' A long pause, but she still couldn't find any other words. 'It's over.'

'Celia,' he said, pressing her hand, 'I wish I could say I'd never see August again, but I have to be truthful to you, I can't. She meant a lot to me, and I can't stop seeing her. But it won't be often. We hardly see each other above twice a year. You know how it is – we're both busy filming. She lives in Los Angeles now, and I live in London. It's only on accidental occasions like this – '

'Max,' she interrupted him firmly, 'I don't think you're getting the point. I'm not asking you for anything. I *know* you can't drop her, that's why I know that whatever it was we were having – an affair, if you like – is finished.'

He stared at her. 'You really mean it, don't you?' She nodded.

'I thought at first that it was something permanent, but I see now that it was only ever a passing – '

'No,' he said fiercely. 'Whatever you think of me, you must believe that I meant it when I said I love you. I do love you. But you're too good for me. You know, I used to tease you about thinking actors were a race apart. But I think you were right. They are. Everything bad you ever thought about a film actor is true about me.'

'Oh darling, don't,' Celia said.

'No, it's true. I tell lies, I play parts, I hardly ever really mean what I say. Sometimes I don't even know what I mean to mean. I seek glory, I crave attention. If I don't get it, I sulk. Christ, I *know* I'm like that. I see myself doing it, just as if I'm watching myself on a film. But one part of me wasn't acting with you, Celia. I meant it when I said I loved you. Please believe that.'

'I believe it,' she said, because he seemed to need the reassurance. Whether she did believe it or not was something she would have to ask herself when she was alone and at leisure.

He went on. 'I had a rotten childhood. My parents hated each other, and when they split up they used me as a weapon. I suppose that's why I am the way I am. I don't know if I became an actor because I was like that – maybe the profession attracts people like it. But I fitted in. And then people wanted me. They hung around me, and flattered me, and did whatever I said. A real ego-trip, you know, but satisfying. August was like that too. We understood each other. But she was stronger, and in the end she wanted me to worship her, and wouldn't give me my turn.' He made a wry face, acknowledging how petty it all was. 'And when I wouldn't bow down, she divorced me. I hated that. It was like my parents all over again. And I can never get rid of the feeling that I can get her back somehow. I hate her really, but she fascinates me. She's so *evil*; like Milton's Satan, tremendously attractive because of it. But you – ' He lifted her hand to his mouth and kissed it, and rubbed his cheek against it, his eyes never leaving her face. Celia trembled at his touch, but kept hold of herself, saying nothing.

'But you, my darling,' he went on. 'The first time I saw you, I thought you were marvellous. I wanted you, and you gave me such a cold shoulder, it made me want you twice as much. But I never thought I'd see you again. I didn't know who you were or anything. And then when you came and rigged up that meeting, I was terribly disappointed. I thought you were just another glory seeker and that I could have you for the taking. But of course, you soon told me that wasn't the case. You gave me the brush-off again, and that time I really knew I had to have you.'

'Don't,' she said. 'Don't talk about it now.' He paid no attention.

'You gave me a hard time, little Celia, but I got you at last, and, oh God, you were marvellous.' He shuddered, kissing her hand again, as if the memory of that physical pleasure were painful to him. 'But it wasn't only the sex, darling, it was you – your lovely cool, certain mind. You seemed to know exactly what you wanted and where you were going. You knew with absolute certainty what was right and what was wrong and which you were going to do. You even sinned with a kind of righteous certainty.' He laughed. 'No wonder I loved you. I do love you still. I don't want to let you go. I won't let you go.' Fierce again, pressing her hand until she could almost bear the pain no longer. The waiter came at that moment with her breakfast, and placed it before her with a curious look at them both.

Celia gently drew her hand away from Max, and began to butter a slice of toast, not because she really wanted it, but to give her something to do, something to prevent her having to meet his eyes. He was still staring at her in a troubled way, she knew, and at last he said, as if he had made up his mind to initiate some desperate remedy, 'Celia, what is it you want? What do you want me to do? Or to promise?' She didn't answer at once, wondering how to. He went on, 'Is it marriage? Do you want me to marry you? I will, if that's the only way to keep you.'

She met his eyes now; it was necessary; and he must have read her reply in her face, for his lips trembled even before she spoke. 'No, Max,' she said. 'I wouldn't want to marry you on those terms. I don't even know if I would marry you if it was what *you* wanted. I don't see it as a last resort, you see. And I don't think I could marry a man who thought I was too good for him. I'd want him to think that he was the only man good enough for me.

He looked at her for a moment more, and then slowly stood up. His face was set. He gave a half-smile that looked as though it had been forced out despite great pain, and leaning over he kissed her lightly on the forehead and without a word walked out of the room. It was probably the best exit of his long career.

THIRTEEN

Looking back on it afterwards, Celia often wondered how she'd had the strength of character to survive those last months when the crew returned to England for the studio-filming. Added to the problem of being so close to Max and desiring him still, had been a new element – pity. He seemed genuinely to suffer from her withdrawal; perhaps it had been nearer to the truth than either of them guessed when he had said he loved her.

Max's behaviour wavered like an unsound compass from coldness, almost rudeness, through languishing, to over-familiarity. He did everything he could to coax, entice or bully her back into his bed, and she was often at her wits end as to how to meet his various approaches without succumbing simply through a desire for peace. That she did hold on, she knew, was largely thanks to Simon. He did all he could to keep her away from Max, finding her jobs which would send her away from the studios, and doing many of her jobs himself while she did his.

He also gave her his silent, sympathetic, and constant support during working hours, and did his best to fill her leisure hours so that Max would not have the opportunity to badger her, and she would not have the opportunity to repine. Thanks to Simon's support, she managed to deal with Max throughout with a neutral friendliness and politeness, however extravagant his approaches to her, and to retain that which she needed most of all, a sense of her own dignity.

Between her and Simon a far better understanding and closer relationship developed, starting on that Sunday afternoon when he took her out in a boat across the jewel-blue Aegean to look at some islands. The boat dropped them at Hydra for an hour-and-a-half stop, and they turned their backs on the waiting embrace of the tourist traps and went down to the rocky shore of the island and bathed.

The water was as mild as milk, scarcely cooler than their skin, and so exquisitely clear that even when they were out of their depth they could see every stone and shell on the sea-bottom with extraordinary, magnified clarity. Celia and Simon swam out side

146

by side, neither touching nor talking, and bobbed among the small waves for a while looking at the white steamer kissing her still reflection in the water, and the alien sea-birds moving about smoothly in the impossibly blue sky like fish in a lake; then they swam back to the shallows, and lounged there against the rocks, talking.

They talked a bit about Max. Bit by bit Celia knew she would tell him everything; he had a calm way of listening, not looking at her all the time, but nodding carefully from time to time so that she knew he was not miles away but right there with her. And when he did look at her, his fine, firm face and frank eyes held no criticism, no censorship. Celia felt that she could tell him anything, anything, and that he would never judge her. Nothing she could say or do would make him feel any differently about her, and it made her feel marvellously safe and secure.

Because safe and secure were things she hadn't felt. 'In some ways I'm like Max,' she told him. 'I see bits of me in him. My parents split up, you know. They actually had the distinction of doing it twice - they divorced and remarried, and then separated again, and they would have got divorced a second time only they got killed before they could make it to the court.' She could say this, knowing it would not be seen as a plea for sympathy. 'Max said that neither of his parents wanted him, while both mine wanted me, but in the end it came down to the same thing. He said his parents used him as a weapon, and so did mine.'

At another time she said, 'I'm a chronic case - I want a permanent relationship, but I don't believe they can exist.'

'Do you believe you are incapable of a permanent relationship, or that other people are?' Simon asked her.

'I wonder,' she said. 'I think I could love someone well enough; and if I could, other people ought to be able to. I suppose I must think that the times are against us.'

He did not ask her which *us* she was referring to, which was as well because she probably would not have known. Then it was her turn to ask and be told - she wanted to know how Simon had managed to reach his advanced age without being married. She knew underneath that part of what she was asking was *are you a homosexual?* but because she already knew in her heart that he was not, she could not phrase the question that way.

He rolled over on to his back in the water, looking away from her up at the sky, and told her, 'I was married, a long time ago,' he said. 'We were both very young – I was sixteen, she was only fifteen – it was before the law was changed in Scotland. That's where I come from.'

'I didn't know. You don't have an accent.'

'I haven't been back for a long time. I don't go there much, if I can help it. It brings back too many memories.'

'Unhappy ones?'

He glanced at her. 'Yes. We weren't happy. Her parents didn't want her to marry me, but she was pregnant. so they had to let it go ahead. It wasn't my baby, but we let them think it was. I thought I was in love with her – very young and romantic – and she was frightened and wanted to get away from home. So young as we were, it was hopeless.' Celia waited, not daring even to breathe loudly in case it disturbed him. He went on. 'Not long after we were married the silly frightened girl went and got herself an abortion. Such things could be arranged in Edinburgh in some of the back streets. Her parents were well-off and gave her more money than was good for her. She was very ill, almost died. She was in hospital for a long time, and ill at home for a long time after that. She told me she didn't want to have sex with me in case she conceived again – birth control was not so easy or so certain in those days. I was young enough not to see through her, until she came to me frightened out of her wits because she was pregnant again.'

'Was it the same man?'

'I don't know. I believe so. I don't think she was really promiscuous. She tried to get it aborted again, but it didn't work, and she had to go through with it. After that she started to drink, and take drugs, and all sorts of stupid things.'

He spoke in a normal tone of voice, but Celia could see that he still felt the pain by the tightening of his lips.

'In the end she killed herself while under the influence of drugs. She borrowed her father's car, and drove it out to South Queensferry and parked it facing the water. She ran a length of hose-pipe from the exhaust through the window and turned the engine on.' A brief silence. 'She wasn't quite eighteen.'

'What happened to the child?' Celia asked after a while.

'Her parents took it and brought it up. He has my name, but he isn't my child after all. I've never seen him.' He looked at Celia. 'You think that's wrong? I couldn't bear it at first; later – there seemed no point in disturbing his life again.'

'And you've never wanted to marry again?'

'I never wanted anyone to take the risk. I've envied Bill often enough, but – I suppose I felt like a kind of Jonah. Maybe if I hadn't married her, she wouldn't have come to that in the end.'

'What was her name?' Celia asked. 'You just call her *she*.'

'I only ever think of her as *she*,' he said with a smile. 'Her name was Antonia. Her parents wanted her to be a boy, you see. From birth, she got everything wrong.'

Impulsively, Celia reached out to touch his hand, but stopped herself before he had seen the gesture. It was his story, not hers. Cautiously she said, 'Christopher Shalako spent a lot of time and energy trying to convince me that you were homosexual.'

'Did he? I'm not surprised.' He looked at her to see if he had succeeded, saw that he hadn't, and went on. 'I suppose it's what a lot of people would assume, seeing a bachelor of my age. I knew Boris, and when Chris got into trouble a few years back I did what I could to help. He came to me and said he wanted to get out of dancing and into films, and I thought the change would be beneficial for him, and helped him again. I gave him a part in one of my films, and of course while it was being filmed I saw a lot of him. He came into my hotel room one night when we were on location and tried to get into bed with me.'

Celia waited. 'Is that all?' she asked at last, when it seemed he was not going to say any more. His blue eyes met hers with transparent enquiry.

'What does that enigmatical question mean?' he asked. 'Is that all? Not all of Chris's story, if that's what you mean. I suppose I wasn't firm enough in my refusals. I felt sorry for the boy; perhaps I should have been more brutal. Perhaps he still harbours hope. Does he still think I will love him?'

'I don't think so,' Celia said carefully. 'I think he wanted to put me off you, that's all. He obviously thinks very highly of you.'

'That's nice to know,' he said ironically.

'But why did you give him a part in this film?'

'*I* give him a part?'

Celia blushed. 'Well, I know it's Walter's choice, but didn't you put him up to it?'

'Yes, I did. Sharp girl. Boris asked me to. He wanted Chris out of the way. Apparently he's been hanging round Toby, and Boris doesn't want any trouble.'

'Oh,' Celia said. 'What tangled lives everyone seems to lead.'

'Not quite everyone,' Simon said, smiling reassuringly at her. 'There are some people whose lives are splendidly straightforward. Whenever I feel, like you, that there are too many sorrows of man's own making in the world, I get myself invited to Bill's house for a meal. To see him with his wife and children is literally a tonic. I go home afterwards feeling soothed and invigorated.'

'Maybe I should try that,' Celia said.

'Maybe. Maybe you can even do better for yourself than that.'

She had no time to discover what that meant, for at that moment the steamer's warning siren was sounded, and they had only ten minutes to get themselves dried and dressed and back to the boat.

On other occasions when they talked, she heard the rest of Simon's story, how he came to get into films after drifting from one job to another for several years, and so on. Everything she learned about him increased her feeling of pleasure in his company. She had the impression that few people were favoured with as much of his confidence.

It turned out to be a year of pretty unremarkable films, no *Jaws* or *Star Wars* coming out of America to break records, no trendsetters to clog the markets with sequels, prequels and imitations. *The Athens Affair* seemed to get better and better as it went on, and by the time the advance publicity was going out the critics were already picking out its good points and the pundits were talking about possible Oscars. Simon was modestly hopeful. Walter's direction had turned a mediocre script into something very much more subtle and meaningful even than the writer had intended; but the news that it had been chosen for the Royal Première made him shake his head.

'Films never get awards when they've been the Royal Première. It's a death-stroke to any artistic achievement.'

'Nonsense,' Celia told him briskly. 'If the film's got it, nothing can kill it.' Simon only laughed and patted his cheek.

'It would be nice if we lived in a world where merit alone was rewarded. Still, it should be a box-office success, and we need that as much as anything. After all, no money, no backers; and no backers, no more money.'

Whatever Simon's feelings, Celia was thrilled to bits to be

attending the Première, more especially so since she would have a prominent place there, would be escorted by Simon himself, and introduced to the Queen. She spent a large lump of her savings on a dress for the occasion, because though she had some lovely clothes she felt none of them was fine enough for a Royal occasion.

'We'll have to go by taxi,' Simon said. 'There won't be anywhere to park there, even if it were thinkable to walk up to the doors dressed as we'll be dressed. What I'll do is order a taxi from my flat, and pick you up in it, all right? I wish we could go in your lovely DB, but – '

'I don't think I could drive my lovely DB. I'll be as nervous as a tic.'

Simon collected her at six, and rang at her doorbell looking unfamiliar and handsome and strangely young in evening-dress.

'You ought always to wear it,' she told him. 'You look really – fine!'

'I have no words to describe how you look,' he said looking her up and down with an expression almost of awe. 'I feel immensely proud to be escorting you. You are really beautiful.'

'Thank you,' Celia said with a slight blush. Her new dress was a Lanvin, of pure silk, a deep turquoise in colour and with a very simple line except for the beautiful flowing sleeves. The bodice was decorated with tiny crystal droplets that shimmered as she moved, and the upper part of the sleeves was slashed with silver chiffon. She had had her hair done that morning in a Mayfair salon, piled around her head like downy clouds so that the fairest pieces showed, and it looked almost silver by artificial light. Round her neck she wore the little jade dolphin Max had given her. Simon offered her his arm, and she walked beside him like a queen, happy and excited and proud.

The evening went like a dream. At the cinema there was a canopy over the door and a carpet across the pavement along which Simon and Celia walked through banked crowds on either side, while cameras clicked and flashed at them. The doorman saluted and did not even glance at the invitations Simon handed over – he recognized him, as a good doorman should. Inside the foyer under the dazzling chandeliers were gathered more celebrities than you could shake a stick at. Celia was absorbed with putting names to them, wishing there was someone to whom she could cry excitedly, 'Oh look, there's so-and-so!' But of course

Simon was one of the celebrities himself, and people were saying *that* about him.

Walter was there with his wife, and came over to greet them and congratulate them and be congratulated by them. All the cast were there, and Simon had a few words for each of them, right down to the last extra. There were a number of other film stars there for the occasion, many of whom knew Simon personally and some of whom had a few kind words for his dazzled assistant. Celia saw Chris in the distance, and Boris and Toby, but could not get through to say hello. She also saw August Dane, on the arm of a very young man in a white dinner-jacket; and Max Prior, much fêted, apparently accompanying Fern Hastings and surrounded by interviewers and television cameras.

Then they were all lined up; the Queen arrived, and walked down the line being introduced to each of them. Celia was glad that she had been taught how to curtsey at school – some of the women made a wretched job of it. The Queen stopped to talk to Simon, and had obviously liked his other work for she had quite a bit to say to him. To Celia she said only, 'Good evening', but it was enough. It was the proudest moment of her life so far, to be presented to the Queen on such an occasion.

And then at last they were in the darkened auditorium, and the film was beginning. The credits rolled, the opening sequences, and then the film she had lived with from script to celluloid was unrolling in front of her eyes, a finished product at last. It was far, far better in its entirety than she had expected, thanks mainly to Walter's directing and the acting of the three principals. Max, particularly, got a strength of emotion out of what were essentially banal situations that made Celia completely revise her estimate of his acting ability. Fern was perfect for her part, truly sweet and innocent without being saccharine, and Chris gave the villain an extra dimension of wry humour which made it quite plausible that Fern should fall in love with him.

When the riding scene came on, and Celia saw herself at a distance cantering down beside the trees, she really at first wondered if it *was* her, for wrapped up in the story she felt it really must be Madeleine, i.e. Fern. Then the terrific camera-work that turned her fall into something quite spectacular and made some of the audience gasp, and there was Max kissing the fallen heroine with unmistakable passion, and Celia's heart gave an uncomfortable lurch. That was where it had all begun. Perhaps guessing her thoughts, Simon reached out for her hand at that point and squeezed it, and unaccountably forgot to let it go all through the rest of the film.

There was a party afterwards, and it was obvious from the attitudes of everyone, including the press, that the film was going to be a success. Fern and Max were surrounded again. Fern was hailed as a new star, and gossip columnists were getting photos of the two together with a view to working up a column on their new romance. Celia thought of August Dane and Rain Bacchus and Max himself, and ended up feeling sorry for Fern. She hoped Fern had a man of her own, for if she was available, she would find it hard to resist Max's charm.

'Charlie Mandelbaum rides again,' she said aloud. Simon, beside her, looked down with a crook of the eyebrow.

'Sorry?'

'Nothing. Just reminiscing.'

Simon studied her for a moment. 'Want to go home?'

'I think so,' she said. 'Can we?'

'We aren't what they want,' he said. 'Fern and Max and Walter are their prey for tonight. No on cares about a stuffy old producer. Have you had enough champagne?'

'Oh yes. It wasn't very good champagne.'

'It never is. It's one of life's disillusionments, that no one who serves enough champagne ever serves a good one, and no one who serves a good champagne ever gives you enough of it. Come on, little one, I'll take you home.'

He would have left her at the door of her house, but she asked him to come in, insisted, in fact.

'Please come in and have some coffee. I'm sure you need it – I certainly do.'

'All right,' he said in the end, 'but could you make it tea? I'm devilishly thirsty.'

'Would you really rather have tea?' Celia smiled with pleasure. 'I would too, but it sounds so unsophisticated to offer at this time of night.'

'I'm an unsophisticated person,' Simon said firmly, 'as you'll discover when you come to know me better.'

'I do know it already,' she said 'It's one of the things I like about you. Put some music on, and I'll bring it through.'

When she came back a little while later with the tea-tray, he had put on the corner lamps and a Tchaikovsky record – the Second Symphony.

'Unusual choice,' she said. 'But right for now.'

'I'm glad you approve.' He waited until she had poured the tea and settled down on the end of the sofa opposite him and then said, 'When you said it was one of the things you like about me, doesn't that imply there are others?'

'Of course,' she said. 'Any number of them. I like you immensely. I couldn't work for you so happily if I didn't.'

'Do you think you could work, not for me, but with me, as happily?' He didn't let her answer, but went straight on, looking at his hands which held his teacup. 'You see, I have been thinking a lot recently that I'd like to try my hand at directing. It seems a natural progression.'

'Directing? But that's wonderful! You know, I've thought so often recently that that's what you ought to be doing. You'd do it so well!'

He looked up now. 'You think so? I'm glad. I'd certainly like to try. But it means someone else will have to do my job as producer – most of it, anyhow. The only person I'd really trust with the job is you.'

Celia had no words, but her shining eyes told him she accepted. He put his teacup aside and stood up, and began to walk about the room, uncharacteristically nervous. 'There is one other thing, though,' he said.

'It sounds like an objection,' she said, 'from your tone of voice.'

'It might be. I hope it isn't. I truly hope it isn't,' he said earnestly. 'You see, the thing is, though you are the person I want to do the job, I don't know whether I could continue to work with you in the present circumstances.' She stared at him, surprised and almost hurt.

'What do you mean?'

'Celia,' he went on hastily, 'the thing is, I don't know whether you've noticed – God, I'm making a bad job of this. Frankly, I'm finding it very difficult to concentrate when you're around. Very difficult to keep my hands off you.'

Celia was now very pale. She too put her cup aside, tea untasted. She stared at him wordlessly.

'You've never played anything but fair with me – I don't mean to suggest it – but I've come to care for you a very great deal. In fact, I've been in love with you almost since the first day I saw you. I don't think I can go on much longer as I am.'

Celia stood up, her instinctive desire to go to him and comfort him. She saw the genuine trouble in his face. In her high-heeled evening slippers she was of a height with him. She stood before him, and he touched her shoulders lightly with hands that trembled uncontrollably. She put her own hands round his waist, and instantly his desire flamed up. He pulled her to him frantically, pressing his mouth to her hair, murmuring incoherent snatches of phrases into her ear while his whole body trembled at the touch of her.

'Celia, I don't know how to ask you this without it sounding like blackmail, but I want you with me for always, to work with me and live with me both. Will you marry me?'

She waited for a long time before answering, so long that his heart sank. Then she said, 'Does it have to be marriage?'

He found the strength to put her back from him to arm's length, and studied her face seriously. 'Not if you don't want it,' he said gently. 'But I'm an old-fashioned sort of lover, and I wouldn't want to share you with anyone. I'd like to do everything properly and above-board, so that no one could ever point the finger at either of us, and so that everyone would know I love you more than anyone or anything in the world. That's why I want to marry you. But if you didn't want it, you wouldn't need to be afraid. I would never leave you, married or not, unless you sent me away.'

She looked at him, and there were tears in her eyes. Her lips moved once or twice, but no sound came out.

'What's your objection to marrying?' he asked her at last. 'Or do you just not want me? Don't be afraid to speak the truth. You know I could never blame you.'

'It was only, I didn't want to give up my job,' Celia said at last, rather incoherently. Simon looked at her intently, and then almost laughed.

'Dearest, did you think I'd make you stay home and wash socks? What kind of a man do you take me for? No, I want you to work beside me, to work with me. I want us to be a team, an equal partnership, making films together. Our life's work, if you like.' He drew her a little closer. 'But, does that mean that you

155

might consider my proposition? That you don't find me completely repulsive.'

She gave a shaky sigh that turned into a laugh. 'Simon, you *know* – ' She was trembling too. She closed the gap between them to nothing, put her arms up round his neck, pressed her body against him. 'You must know by now – '

'Yes,' he said. He kissed her lightly on the lips, lingeringly on each eye, and paused above her lips again like someone putting off to the last moment some almost unendurable delight. 'I think I do. Thank God you do feel like this. It would have killed me to see you go to someone else. Celia, I love you so much, I wouldn't trust any other man to make you happy.'

They stood together, mouth to mouth, in the dimly lit room, the tide of passion rising in each of them. Soon they would have to do something about it; and Celia was happily aware that this time the ebb would not leave them stranded, but would take them with it; that for the rest of their lives together it would be the element they lived in, their natural place.